"Ophelia, what was your objective with that confrontation at lunch?"

She fiddled with the cloth she picked up from the countertop. "I let myself hope."

"Hope?" he repeated.

Her need to make him understand shocked her. "That maybe you'd wake up and see that what you think you want isn't how it has to be."

"You mean us? It wouldn't work Ophelia." His head moved in a slow back-and-forth sideways.

"I'm all wrong for you. I'm too old."

"You're not that old," she protested. Opie meant what she'd told Val about age. She didn't care that Wendell was older than her.

"We're too different in all the ways that count."

"How can you know that? Do you really know me?" she asked, staring at him.

"I know your values. I know what you want out of life. It wouldn't work."

"You think you know me so well, but you don't," she argued, turning away from him.

"I know you better than you realize. I know you'd never do anything to hurt your family, which would happen if you became involved with an old sinner like me."

TERRY FOWLER is a native Tar Heel who loves calling coastal North Carolina home. Single, she works full-time and is active in her small church. Her greatest pleasure comes in the way God has used her writing to share His message. Her hobbies include gardening, crafts, and genealogical research. Terry invites everyone to visit her webpage at terryfowler.net.

Books by Terry Fowler

HEARTSONG PRESENTS

HP298—A Sense of Belonging
HP346—Double Take
HP470—Carolina Pride
HP537—Close Enough To Perfect
HP629—Look to the Heart
HP722—Christmas Mommy
HP750—Except for Grace
HP793—Coming Home
HP841—Val's Prayer
HP862—Heath's Choice

Opie's
Challenge

Terry Fowler

Heartsong Presents

To God be the glory—thank You for helping me confront
the challenge of writing these stories.

To Mary and Steve with love—
thanks for showing me your Kentucky.

To my family—I love you all.

And as always, a special thank you to
Mary and Tammy for their help.

A note from the Author:
I love to hear from my readers! You may correspond with
me by writing:

Terry Fowler
Author Relations
PO Box 721
Uhrichsville, OH 44683

ISBN 978-1-60260-676-0

OPIE'S CHALLENGE

All scripture quotations are taken from the King James Version of the
Bible.

Our mission is to publish and distribute inspirational products offering
exceptional value and biblical encouragement to the masses.

PRINTED IN THE U.S.A.

one

"Okay, ladies, get ready. Our final bachelor of the evening is every woman's dream man. Not only does he embody the three *Hs* of Paris—horses, history, and hospitality—he's a handsome hottie looking for his number one lady." The female emcee's breathy voice filled the room, "Wendell Hunter, come on out!"

"Could she use one more *H* word?" Ophelia Truelove's sarcasm gained her a look of disbelief from her sister. She shrugged and grinned.

"Wendell owns our own Hunter Farm right here in Paris. He's looking for the woman whose focus is her family and home."

While the woman extolled his virtues, he walked out onto the runway. Opie wanted to claim he strutted like a peacock but in truth, he moved with the confidence of a man comfortable in his own skin. Wendell Hunter definitely looked as good in real life as he had in the photographs she'd seen in the article that had given Val the idea to attend the bachelor auction.

He might not be handsome by most standards, but possessed a magnetism that attracted women. He wore his dark brown hair short, probably to control the curl. His heavy-lidded eyes and chiseled cheekbones belied a serious expression that didn't match the frivolity of the evening, and yet he'd smiled easily enough earlier when mingling among the women in his effort to raise more money for tonight's event.

Given their rapt expressions and the way the women leaned forward in their seats, Opie knew there would be more than one taker in this room. Too bad his viewpoints regarding women's rights were rooted years in the past. Opie admitted the comments in his interview influenced her regard for

Wendell Hunter. When Val asked what she was reading a few days earlier, she'd shown her the article was on Paris's most eligible bachelors. Val laughed and asked if they really had any.

"Yeah, they're having a bachelor auction fund-raiser. Look at this guy," Opie said, pointing to the page. "Wendell Hunter. He believes a woman's sole focus should be her family and home. That's so antediluvian."

"Hunter?" Val reached for the magazine. "That's my architect's brother."

Her eyebrows shot up in surprise. "Small world."

"How would you like to go to a bachelor auction?"

Opie couldn't believe her ears. Val never wasted money on frivolous activities. "Are you nuts?"

"No. I just thought it might be fun to check out Paris's most eligible bachelors."

"You want to check out your architect's brother."

"I do," she admitted.

"I don't think seeing Wendell Hunter strut the runway is going to give you much insight."

"I don't know. It might tell us more than you know. I'll buy you a new dress," Val offered. When Opie hesitated, she said, "Shoes, too."

"Okay, I'm in," Opie agreed. "But you have to buy something for yourself, as well."

They went shopping and tonight when she dressed for this event, Opie experienced second thoughts. Though she told herself they were just going to look, Opie feared it wouldn't be that simple.

While Wendell wanted a woman whose sole focus was her husband, children, and home, Opie considered the woman's role in today's world had changed. Most women obtained their education with the intention of having a career in their chosen fields. Opie looked forward to using her bachelor's degree in culinary management to achieve her life goals.

A father who worked full-time to provide for his family's needs and a stay-at-home mother had raised Opie and her six siblings. Her dad loved his job, but she often wondered if her mother had been as fulfilled with her choice. Perhaps being a mother and wife was enough for some women but not for Opie.

Given his financial status, she doubted Wendell needed a working wife. She couldn't see any place in his plan for career women. Women had come from not being able to vote to a run for the White House, but they'd never get there if they allowed men with viewpoints like his to stand in the way of their progress.

"Hey, what do you think you're doing?" Opie demanded when Val grabbed her paddle and started the bidding war. Aware that women around them watched with interest, she discreetly tried to catch Val's hand as she outbid each woman in quick succession until the auctioneer declared number 230, Ophelia Truelove, the winner.

"Have you lost your mind?" Opie hissed.

Val smiled easily. "I bought you a date."

Opie glowered at her. "This isn't funny, Val."

"It's a good cause."

She crossed her arms and declared, "I won't go."

Val shrugged. "Like I said, it's a good cause. The scholarship fund gets the money regardless of whether you take advantage of the opportunity."

"Why would you do that?" Opie couldn't say why she felt so humiliated.

"You liked what you saw in that magazine. Besides, you have something to say to Mr. Hunter and after the way you went on about his interview, I thought it might take you a couple of hours to share your opinion."

A lifetime probably wouldn't be long enough. His statements irritated her, but she did find him to be handsome. She'd never admit that to Val. "All I said was I couldn't believe how old-fashioned he was."

"I think the word was antediluvian. Where do you come up with those words anyway?"

She glanced around and slouched in her chair when she noted several sets of eyes watching them. Some looked curious, others positively angry. Most probably wondered who they were and where they got the money to buy a date with the prize bachelor of the evening.

"There's nothing wrong with improving your vocabulary," she muttered.

Val indicated Wendell Hunter when he stepped into the room and moved in their direction. "Here comes your opportunity."

"You know I won't say anything," Opie mumbled, wishing she could sink into the floor.

"Why? Afraid you'll embarrass yourself?"

Opie's displeasure showed in her narrowed gaze and unfriendly look. "I'm already embarrassed. This is ridiculous, Val. I've never done anything like this to you."

While she admitted to her fair share of pranks on her older sister, she didn't recall ever putting Val in such an embarrassing position. Wondering if she had time to make her getaway, Opie glanced up to find Wendell Hunter only steps away.

Lack of self-esteem was not this man's problem. Even at average height, he would tower over her five foot two inch height. The expensive tuxedo and carefully styled hair made him appear very different from the men she knew. She doubted he'd ever worn a baseball cap or a cowboy hat. Of course, thus far the men in her life consisted of a couple of old boyfriends, her father and brothers, male farm employees, and the chefs she came across in the course of her work.

He stopped before them and looked at Val. "You're Ophelia?"

She shook her head. "I'm Val Truelove." She pointed to her sister. "This is Ophelia."

Recognition dawned in his gaze. "You own Sheridan Farm?"

"Yes," Val agreed with a pleased smile.

He extended his hand. "Welcome to the neighborhood."

"We've been in the neighborhood since Val was a toddler," Opie said coolly. How could he live just down the road and not know they existed? Then again, if she were fair, she hadn't really known about him either. "I'm Opie. Our father managed the farm for the Sheridans."

His dark eyebrows shot up. "Jacob Truelove is your father?"

"He is," Val said before Opie could comment.

"I've met him. Mr. Sheridan always spoke very highly of your father." He focused brilliant blue eyes on Opie and said, "It's a pleasure to meet you, Ophelia. Would you care to hear what I have planned for our date?"

His formal pronunciation of her name immediately caught her attention. The name had been the bane of her existence for as long as Opie could remember. She gladly exchanged it for a nickname even if it did sound a little tomboyish.

She wanted to say no, but yes tumbled out before she could stop herself. The mystery in his eyes beckoned to her. She purposefully turned away from Val's knowing grin and concentrated on the man before her.

"I thought we would have dinner at my home," he began, smiling when he added, "If you like French cuisine, my chef is excellent."

Of course he'd have a French chef. No doubt imported straight from France. Only the best for men like Wendell Hunter. "My father wouldn't approve of me being alone with you in your home."

He didn't miss a beat. "We wouldn't be alone. My staff would be there the entire time. Or you could invite your sister along." Again, he flashed Val a friendly smile.

Could things get any worse? she wondered, feeling her cheeks grow hot. Did he feel the need to provide her with a protector or was he interested in Val? No doubt the women who came to his home didn't require a chaperone. In fact, she knew that most women in this room wouldn't want anyone around if they had an opportunity to be alone with him. "No, that won't be necessary. Your staff will be sufficient."

Opie didn't know that she'd find the nerve to comment on his article, but she didn't need witnesses along on the date.

Wendell named a date and time, and Opie accepted his business card. "I'll check my calendar and get back to you," she said.

His smile softened his otherwise austere features. He dipped his head slightly and said, "It's truly been my pleasure, ladies. Please accept my undying gratitude for saving me from the embarrassment of being left standing on the runway."

That certainly hadn't been the case. Other women flashed those paddles as determinedly as Val in their pursuit of the date. Opie didn't doubt for one moment that he knew that.

"I'm sure the ladies are very appreciative of your contribution to their fund-raising efforts," Opie offered, sharing her own saccharine-sweet smile.

᚛

At home, Wendell shed the jacket and tie on the way to his office. He'd been negotiating the purchase of a stallion prior to the event and wanted to check his progress. Tonight had proved interesting. Participating in a bachelor auction, even for a charitable cause, wasn't something he wanted to do, but his longtime friend persisted until he agreed.

The young woman who bought his date definitely caught his attention. Ophelia Truelove was his type. He had a decided leaning toward beautiful, petite blond-haired women with expressive green eyes. She'd surprised him with her sarcastic reply to his welcome and became prickly when she shared that they were the daughters of the former manager of Sheridan Farm. The Trueloves now owned the farm and if what he'd seen on the news and read was fact, their wealth equaled or exceeded that of a number of people in Bourbon County. At least Val Truelove's did.

When introducing himself, Wendell noted the two women seemed at odds. At first, he feared he'd become embroiled in some sort of feud. Both women held paddles and yet Catherine pointed out Val as the winning bidder. Had they competed for his date? He didn't think so. Val Truelove quickly pointed out her sister as the winner.

He found Ophelia Truelove to be a bit of a contradiction.

Outspoken but sheltered if what she'd said about her father objecting to her coming to his home alone was true. Still, she'd rejected his suggestion that she bring her sister. Evidently, it would be okay so long as they weren't alone in the house.

He'd have to instruct his staff to remain that evening. Everyone but Jean-Pierre. The chef would leave as soon as he completed service. He prepared incredible food, but Wendell found his temperament less than desirable. Then, what else did one expect of a French chef? Jean-Pierre impressed his business associates and that pleased Wendell. He'd put up with artistic temperament for that.

As for the date, Catherine reminded him before the auction that it was only one night out of his life for a good cause. Wendell considered that spending a few hours in a beautiful woman's company for a good cause couldn't be all bad. Pushing the evening from his thoughts, he sat down at his desk and pulled up his e-mail on the laptop. A pleased smile changed his expression when he read that he now owned a new stallion.

&

Still fuming over Val's prank, Opie said little after they left the event.

"What calendar is it you need to check?" Val teased as they got into the car.

"I didn't care to appear overly eager," Opie offered stiffly as she fastened her seat belt.

"That was fun."

"When did watching men flaunt themselves become fun for you?"

A jangle of keys and the click of her seat belt preceded Val's response, "I appreciate that they're willing to donate their time and efforts for charity. Besides, it was a new experience for us both."

They rode in silence. Opie wanted to be angry but knew her sister intended no harm. Besides, if she hadn't made such a big deal over the article, Val would never have realized he was Russ's brother and this would never have happened.

When Val suggested they attend and threw in the offer of a new dress and shoes, Opie believed she'd gotten the better end of the deal. Instead, she now suffered the consequences of giving in to temptation.

Inviting Russ Hunter to join them for lunch last week started this. Opie knew Val didn't care to spend more time in the young architect's presence, particularly after he'd produced and presented a disappointing set of plans for Val's new business venture that same day.

But Opie needed to know more about Russ Hunter. Even though he did business with Val, she needed to form her own opinion about the man whose plans would bring changes to their longtime home.

She'd also wondered at Val's strong reaction to Russ and thought perhaps there was more to the situation than met the eye. The twins liked Russ and she did, too. She found both Hunter men to be attractive.

"Just tell me why you did it," she said, not yet willing to let the subject drop.

Val sighed. "Because you said you wanted to tell him how you felt."

"Did it occur to you that I didn't actually mean I wanted to give him a piece of my mind?"

"Then why didn't you just say no?"

Because she didn't want to refuse. Thankful for the darkness inside the car, Opie said, "You paid a lot for that date. I didn't want to appear any more stupid than I already felt."

"Why would you feel stupid?"

"Did you really look at him, Val?"

"He seemed a nice enough man."

"Exactly. A very handsome, wealthy man who probably thinks I'm the most immature child he's ever met. I can't believe I told him I couldn't be alone with him in his house."

"You can't. Daddy wouldn't allow it. But why do you care what he thinks?"

Opie wished she had the answer to that one. Maybe she

didn't want to care, but she did. From the first time she saw him in the magazine and even after she'd met him in person, Wendell Hunter captured her attention in a way no other man had ever done. "Because I should be able to do whatever I want."

"Who says you can't?"

"Men like Wendell Hunter."

"There are plenty of men who don't mind working wives, Opie."

"I know, but I feel challenged to help him understand one person shouldn't limit another's possibilities."

"The future Mrs. Hunter will decide whether she wants to fulfill the role he's set forth for her."

"Will she?" Opie demanded. "What about love? What happens when a woman is attracted to a man with this kind of thought process?"

"They decide what they're willing to give up for love."

"Like Mom did?"

"I don't think Mom feels she gave up anything."

Opie believed her mother could do anything, but Cindy Truelove's focus was her husband and children. "Look at her talents, Val. She could do anything she wanted," she argued.

"Or she could do what she did and use those talents in her home to benefit her husband and children and still feel fulfilled."

Opie saw nothing wrong with being career-minded. "How is that possible? What does she have to show for all her effort?"

"A husband and seven children who love her very much."

"Do you honestly believe that's enough?"

"It is for most women. Working outside the home changed our worlds. We spend our days occupied with other responsibilities and then put them aside when we come home. Mom works 24/7. She's every bit as determined to excel as we are in our chosen fields.

"Opie, why are you struggling with this? It's not as if you're in love with Wendell Hunter. He's nearly ten years older than you."

She didn't know why she cared, but she did. "The years don't matter when you meet the right person."

Val braked, slowing down to turn into their driveway. The loud click of the signal indicator filled the sudden silence. "Are you saying you're interested in him?"

"No," Opie declared, stumbling over her hasty denial. "I just meant that an age difference wouldn't hold me back if I met the right man."

"You're a rebel, Opie Truelove. You have problems with people saying you can't do things."

"Daddy says we're determined."

"Stubborn. Determined. Tenacious," Val recited. "Call it what you want. They're all the same."

Opie's defiant nature came to life. "There's nothing wrong with being determined."

"Not as long as you seek God's plan for you. You can't decide your own fate. You can't even steer the ship."

❧

The following afternoon, Opie rifled through the top drawer of her nightstand and removed the magazine she hadn't been able to toss. It opened voluntarily to the exact page. Opie studied Wendell's photo. What did she really know about him? She couldn't say whether he possessed the qualities touted at the auction. She didn't know anything beyond what she'd read and heard and Val's comments regarding Russ's negativity toward his brother. What made him feel as he did about a woman's role in his life?

Had his mother been the ultimate homemaker? Not likely, Opie thought. Considering their wealth, if anything, he'd lived with options she'd never imagined as a child of working-class parents. His mother could have been a socialite. Opie remembered the parties at the Sheridans' mansion. Surely as neighbors with common interests, the Hunters were regulars on their guest list.

Not that she'd ever been there to see who attended. Opie remembered asking her dad why they were never invited. The question generated her first lesson on social status. Despite her father's efforts to make her understand that workers and employers didn't move in the same circles, Opie hadn't understood. Too smart for her own good, she'd reminded him they went to the annual Christmas party.

"Because that party is for the staff," her dad said. "There are places for everyone in this world, Opie. The rich don't rub elbows with the poor." She'd kept on with the questions until he grew tired. He sent her off to ask her mother, who gave her the same answers.

Maybe guaranteed entrée into any party of her choice motivated her to become a chef. She intended to do great things in the culinary world. One day, people would be happy to have Opie Truelove's name on their guest lists.

She considered the pros and cons of accepting the invitation. No reasons to refuse came to mind. He'd even chosen a Tuesday night, which meant she couldn't claim church conflict. Opie glanced at the photo again. She wanted to go out with Wendell Hunter.

When he answered the cell number on his business card, she said, "Hi, it's Opie Truelove. I'm calling about our date."

two

"You eat like this every day?"

Wendell shook his head and chuckled. "This special dinner is in your honor. My way of showing my appreciation for your contribution. Too many of these meals, and my clothes wouldn't fit."

Earlier, when she walked into the drawing room, Wendell couldn't take his eyes off her. She carried herself confidently, wearing a fitted white shirt with a black skirt and high heels that suited her slender, willowy body. He took a few steps forward to accept her hand, noting the short nails nicely buffed to a shine. She smiled, and he stared at her delicate facial features and full lips. Her shiny shoulder-length blond hair framed her face. Definitely his type.

When he signed up for the date, Wendell enlisted Jean-Pierre's help in creating a menu worthy of his charitable contribution. His chef had not let him down. Over canapés of *tapanade* and crab with lemon, Ophelia and Wendell conversed comfortably on a variety of subjects. When offered an aperitif, Ophelia requested tap water.

After moving into the dining room, Wendell watched her eat his favorite, an entrée of *terrine de filets de sole*. Most of his guests ate and enjoyed the food, but she savored every bite. He'd never dined with anyone as expressive as Ophelia. Her auditory sighs and frequent exclamations of praise would make anyone consider her an extreme foodie.

When the server placed the *coq au vin* second course before her, she used her hand to waft the odor and inhaled. Pleasure filled her delicate expression. She tore a piece of french bread from the loaf on her bread plate. "Oh, I'd enjoy this excuse for outgrowing my clothes." She took a bite. "This is wonderful."

Wendell supposed her career choice would be reason enough for her love of food. She'd spoken of her recent graduation from culinary school and plans for the future. "What made you become a chef?" he asked.

"Food is my passion," she offered.

Wendell considered it a trite reason for choosing such a complex career. "Wouldn't most chefs make that claim?"

Ophelia shrugged, tilting her head to the side as she spoke. She pushed the bangs of her silky blond hair from her eyes. "I suppose, but in my case it's true. For as long as I can remember, I've wanted nothing more than to cook. When we were little and Mama ordered us outside so she could prepare a meal, I pleaded with her to let me stay. I pored over cookbooks as if they were great literature, planning the meals that I would one day prepare."

"No toys?" he asked.

"My best-ever Christmas present was a toy oven. Everyone loved my little cakes. Of course, they checked first to make sure they were the real thing and not those dirt cakes I sometimes made when I didn't have ingredients for the others."

He chuckled. "Surely you never got anyone to eat those."

She laughed, shaking her head. "No. They usually threw them at me when they realized what I'd done. Mom taught me to bake when she realized I'd bankrupt them with my supply requests."

Wendell had never known a woman who admitted to making mud pies. Despite his love for the farm, he couldn't claim any special affinity with the soil. "So you've cooked since childhood?"

"Not as often as I would have liked," Ophelia admitted, her focus shifting from the food to him. "I knew early on that I wanted to work with food but had no idea how to get started. When I was fourteen, I cornered one of the Sheridans' caterers. She was up to her eyeballs in hors d'oeuvres and short one of her wait staff. She didn't have time for an inquisitive kid.

"When she asked if I wanted to make a few dollars, I told her I'd rather learn how to prepare the food. She agreed and gave me three or four lessons in exchange for working that night. I picked up quickly, and we worked together for a couple of years."

He nodded, impressed by her willingness to go after what she desired.

"When I got my driver's license, I took a summer job in Paris," she continued. "I convinced the diner owner that I'd rather cook on the grill than serve, and he agreed to let me try. It wasn't easy, but I did it well."

Wendell noted her self-confidence. He'd witnessed that very same characteristic in Jean-Pierre. Wendell appreciated that the chef did his job well even when his bad language and erratic behaviors left something to be desired. "Are you an obnoxious chef?"

She smiled her thanks to the server who replaced her plate with the *salade d'endives, noix et roquefort*, endive salad with walnuts and roquefort cheese. "I suppose I could be if the situation demanded. I don't shout and curse if that's what you mean."

"It's a stressful occupation," he allowed.

"There are ways to overcome the stress."

She ate every bite of the endive salad and dipped her finger into the remaining dressing a couple of times.

Curious about her behavior, he asked, "Would you like more?"

Pushing the plate away, she colored slightly. "Sorry. My mom would tell you my atrocious table manners are an occupational hazard. I was trying to determine what's in the dressing."

He found it intriguing that anyone could identify all the flavors on their plate. "Did you?"

A tiny frown touched her expressive face. "There's a little something extra I can't place."

"Impressive." He sipped his drink. Next Jean-Pierre sent out a cheese plate of Chevretine, Camembert, and Roquefort with baguette slices. "So tell me why they pointed your sister out to me as Ophelia Truelove."

"Val used my paddle to bid on you."

Confused, he asked, "So the date was with her?"

"No, she bought the date for me."

"You mean as a favor?"

She paused and then admitted, "More of a prank."

Aha, he had noticed something between the two of them. In a way, Wendell found their juvenile behavior humorous, but he didn't appreciate feeling used either. "Why would she do that?"

She leaned forward, confiding the truth. "When I first read about you in the magazine, I voiced my opinion about your comments to Val. She had met your brother and said we should attend the auction. Do you truly believe what you said?"

Her reference to Russ caught Wendell by surprise. He had not seen his half brother since their parents' death and found it interesting that he now worked for the Trueloves. "I shared what I'm seeking in a wife so, yes, I do believe that."

"To clean your house and nurture your children?"

Finding her appraisal somewhat insulting, Wendell emphasized, "She would manage our home. The staff would carry out her instructions."

"The staff," Ophelia repeated, almost mocking him. "They have names, you know."

"Yes, I do know. Some have been with me since my childhood."

"What does nurture your children mean?" she persisted. "Give birth and get them walking and talking before shipping them off to heaven only knows where?"

Ophelia's gaze fixed on him. He noted her eyes matched the tiny emerald earrings she wore. Not understanding her determination to dissect him, Wendell answered anyway. "It's loving our children and providing for their needs. And while boarding school is a tradition in my family, that will be a decision we make together."

She nodded. "I thought so. I never saw any reference to you at public school." Before he could comment, Ophelia continued to question him about his personal viewpoints. "What if your wife wants her own career? How would that fit into your plan?"

Exasperated, Wendell said stiffly, "There is no plan. We all have ideas of what we desire in a life partner. I intend to choose carefully."

"How do you find such an ideal partner? It's not as if you can go to the store and pick up the ingredients for the perfect wife. She'll be some woman to meet your stringent requirements."

Her comment angered Wendell. She didn't know him well enough to make that call. He considered his initial assessment of Ophelia. The confidence of youth allowed her to make brash judgments. Though some were right on target, other generalities bothered him.

"So let me get this straight. You're taking this stand against my beliefs for all women?"

She looked perturbed. "No." Before she ducked her head, he caught a glimpse of tightened lips and narrowed gaze. "I can only speak for myself. But I do believe no one should limit another's dreams."

"Surely I'm not the first man you know who made such statements?"

"Well, no."

"Then why do you feel the need for this personal attack?"

Her head dropped. "I don't know." She focused on removing bread crumbs from the tablecloth. "Maybe your interview pushed me over the edge."

"Again, why me?"

"I don't know," she repeated, a distinctive edge to her voice.

"Do you always speak first and apologize later?"

Her head jerked up. "I didn't apologize."

"But you will once you realize how wrong you are."

Her head tilted to the side. "How do you know that?"

"Because your parents taught you right from wrong."

"Is it your turn to analyze me?"

He idly moved his glass as he responded.

"Is that what we've been doing?"

Ophelia sighed heavily. "I only want to understand why you feel as you do."

Wendell wasn't used to explaining himself. "May I ask why?"

"Because I believe women should have the same opportunities as men. No woman should be required to play house and rock babies if she wants more out of life."

She threw down the words like a gauntlet, as if expecting him to battle for his rights. "That's your prerogative Ophelia. Just as believing as I do is my right."

"Surely you knew your date would ask questions based on that article."

Wendell smiled. "Most women aren't so curious." She flushed, and he regretted that he'd embarrassed her. "You obviously came here tonight with your own agenda. I'm thinking that might have been to tell me how outdated you consider me to be."

She grimaced. "That obvious, huh?"

"Let's just say you aren't as practiced in womanly wiles as some of your female counterparts."

Another blush, this time with a rise of spirit. "Nor am I likely to be. I told Val this would be embarrassing. I told you it was a prank, but honestly she saw how irritated I got when I read your article and took me at my word when I said I'd like to give you a piece of my mind. I wondered if you even thought about how you could limit some woman's dreams."

"I would hope her love for me would be the most important factor."

Her icy stare reproved him. "It doesn't bother you that love could stand in the way of your wife's fulfillment?"

"I plan to choose carefully. The woman I marry will want the same things I want in life."

Ophelia shook her head. "Maybe, or it could be her love for you will force her to give up the things that make her happy."

Wendell was attracted to educated, well-spoken women. He'd never ruled out a woman focused on her career. "When you meet the man of your dreams, what happens when your desires clash? Do you say no thanks or try to make the relationship work?"

He could see from Ophelia's expression that he'd made his point.

"I'd try to make it work. I'm sorry, Wendell. My parents would be horrified if they knew how I'd behaved tonight."

The dawning realization in her eyes revealed her distress. "Don't be. I admire your willingness to take on things you don't agree with even if I don't feel my thinking is flawed. My future wife will fulfill a much greater role in my life. She'll be my support, my friend, my confidant, the reason I live. I'll fulfill those same roles for her."

A sad smile touched her expressive face. "And I've wasted your evening by coming here when you could have met that woman instead."

"It's not likely I'd look for the woman of my dreams at a bachelor auction," Wendell said. "I've enjoyed our evening, Ophelia." Her youthful, spirited beauty touched him. Perhaps if she were older or he younger. . . "It is important to consider a woman's expectations of life. You've reminded me not to be selfish."

"I enjoyed this evening, too." Her admission made her smile. "There's so much I want for women, and I wanted you to understand. I've enjoyed seeing your home, too. I remember coming here and thinking how grand it was from the outside. Your mother was leaving and didn't invite me in."

Wendell knew she'd never met his mother. "My mom died before you were born." He could almost see her mind working. "Nicole was Russ's mother. My father's second wife," he explained. "My mother, Meredith, lived at Hunter Farm a brief time."

"Was she sick?"

Wendell didn't like remembering the senseless loss of his mother. Maybe if his father had been around to take care of her, she'd be alive today. "The diagnosis was complications from pneumonia."

"Losing her must have been difficult."

He nodded. "I was three. I don't remember a lot about her."

They concentrated on the meal until Wendell asked, "What were you looking for when you came here tonight, Ophelia?"

"Please stop calling me that. I prefer Opie."

Wendell refused to use the unsuitable tomboyish nickname. He shook his head. "It doesn't fit."

She sighed deeply before answering his earlier question. "I don't know. My future husband will need to understand how important my career is to me. We'll share roles in our home. Whether it's doing chores or raising our children. If we have children. I'm not even sure I want to be a mother."

"No children?" Wendell asked, appalled that she'd consider a career more important than motherhood. "That's a woman's most fulfilling role."

Once more, she rose to the challenge. "How do you know what fulfills a woman? Did whoever raised you with those archaic viewpoints tell you that?"

He didn't much care for her insisting his point of view was ancient. "Why wouldn't you want children?"

"I'm fourth out of seven childern. Right smack in the middle."

He frowned and shrugged. "What does that have to do with becoming a mother? Loving and caring for your siblings is nothing like loving a child you've created with the man you love. A child you've nurtured inside your body." Even as he spoke, Wendell couldn't help but question what qualified him as an expert on the matter. He didn't have children.

"I haven't totally ruled it out. I have a lot to accomplish before I do. I'm only twenty-three."

Wendell thought she sounded a bit defensive. "Ah, I'm thirty-two."

"Men don't have the same problem with biological clocks," she reminded.

"Still, I'd prefer to look like my children's father rather than their grandfather."

She laughed at his droll response, and Wendell enjoyed the pleasant sound.

"Why have you waited so long?"

"Sometimes things don't happen when we want. No matter how differently we plan. So what do you plan for your career?"

"There's a world of possibilities. I've considered opening a restaurant at the farm."

"Why not Paris?" Wendell had heard rumors of plans underway at Sheridan Farm and hated to think what the Trueloves might be planning to do to their peaceful community.

"I think coming to a horse farm would give it a unique flavor. Patrons would be drawn to the glorious scenery."

"It's too much," Wendell declared with a shake of his head. "All those people filling our roads would destroy the ambiance of the area."

Before she could respond, the server entered and asked, "Is there anything else, sir?"

Wendell smiled at the woman and said, "We'll take our dessert and coffee in the drawing room."

"Would you relay my compliments to the chef?" Opie requested when the woman started to leave.

"Please ask Jean-Pierre to join us," Wendell instructed.

Ophelia appeared pleased by his request. When the chef entered the room, she said, "My compliments on the meal. The food was some of the best I've ever eaten. That vinaigrette dressing was out of control. There was a little something I couldn't identify."

"Miss Truelove shares your love of fine cuisine, Jean-Pierre," Wendell said. "She's also a chef."

Something stirred inside when Opie looked at him and smiled, showing he'd pleased her with his acknowledgment.

Jean-Pierre bowed slightly and greeted her, "I'm honored, chef. As for the recipe, my dear *grand-mère* made me promise to keep the secret in the family. But alas, I have no heir."

"It would be mankind's loss that such a fabulous dressing would cease to be served," she countered.

Jean-Pierre's eyes twinkled with merriment. "Ah, not only a beautiful woman but one with a discerning palate. I can see I need to watch my step or you'll charm the recipe right from my lips."

"I can only hope you continue your line," she offered with laughter in her voice. "Otherwise, it will be a terrible loss to the culinary world."

"Perhaps if I do not, I might be tempted to leave my secret to one so lovely as you."

"I would be most honored," she said, flashing him another huge smile.

"We should discuss our mutual love of food at a future time," he suggested.

Ophelia's pleased smile spoke volumes. "I would love to talk food with a fellow chef."

Wendell watched their exchange with interest and experienced a jolt of dissatisfaction at the thought of the two chefs coming together for any reason.

Jean-Pierre bowed slightly. "Again, I thank you, mademoiselle."

"The pleasure was mine. A truly memorable dining experience."

After the pleased chef disappeared back into the kitchen, Wendell pulled back her chair and gestured toward the drawing room across the hall. "I've never heard Jean-Pierre talk that much. Perhaps I should ask for his recipe file. Though I doubt I'd be nearly as successful with my request. He loves his Parisian grandmother a great deal."

She placed her napkin on the table and stood, looking up at Wendell. "Paris, Kentucky to Paris, France. A world away."

"Yes, but we are connected. They renamed our beautiful area to reflect appreciation to the French for their assistance during the Revolutionary War. Would you care to see more of the house?" he asked. "I'm very proud of my home."

"Val said Russ seems particularly fond of the farm as well."

Wendell knew curiosity prompted her to make the comment. "I haven't seen Russ since our parents died. How is he?"

"He seems fine. Family is important, you know."

"Interesting you would say that. It doesn't conform to your plan not to have children."

"I didn't say I wouldn't have a child or two, but they will have a working mother if I do."

Something caught in his chest when an almost flirtatious smile touched her face. He'd have to be careful around this one, Wendell thought, cupping her elbow with his hand. Their conversation over dinner challenged him, and he didn't doubt she could hold her own in any discussion. "Isn't every mother a working mother?"

"You know what I mean."

"I do and I apologize for teasing you. Exactly what is your sister planning?"

She paused to study the portrait hanging in the entry hallway and glanced at him.

"My father," Wendell said.

"You resemble him a great deal. Val's plans are still in early stages, and she's asked us not to discuss them until things are finalized."

"I see."

Wendell led her through the lower floors of the house he'd called home all his years. From the moment he'd welcomed her, Wendell had been aware of her seeking gaze. She'd been outspoken about the home's beauty.

The elegantly decorated drawing room had changed little over the years. Comfortable sofas replaced the antique settees, but most of the home's original features remained. From all accounts, his mother loved those details. Wendell took great comfort in knowing Nicole had not managed to remove Meredith Hunter from the house.

Wendell showed her the library and the sitting room office his mother claimed as her own. While he didn't doubt she'd like to see the upper floor, Wendell knew Ophelia would never ask.

She touched the artfully carved banister as they walked by and said, "These old homes are beautiful."

He nodded agreement and asked, "Do you plan to live in the Sheridan house? It's quite palatial."

"We haven't decided."

Why would they buy such a grand home and not live there? "I always appreciated coming home to this house."

"It's magnificent."

Wendell agreed. "Shall we take our coffee on the porch?"

The porch wrapped around the grand old manor house, overlooking a beautiful garden area. A number of trees hid the working areas of the farm in the distance. The rockers moved easily on the bricked floor as they enjoyed the evening much as previous generations of families had done.

"You'd like the kitchen," he said. "I upgraded to a commercial kitchen when Jean-Pierre agreed to work for me."

"Where did you find him?"

"He worked for an elderly relative. When she died, I talked him into moving to the States."

"I'm sure he appreciates the modernized kitchen. I can hardly wait to have my own. Our kitchen is my mother's domain."

"You mean a restaurant kitchen?"

"Maybe." She shrugged. "I'm not exactly sure what I want to do. I have a million ideas and the list grows daily."

"I thought you wanted a restaurant on the farm?"

She twisted the silver ring on her finger as she spoke. "I want to cook."

"Don't you do that at home?"

"Not like I want. Mom prepares very basic meals. I have to work hard to convince her to allow me to try something new."

Why would a mother send her daughter to culinary school and not allow her to cook at home? "But you're trained. Why wouldn't she want you to prepare the dishes you've learned?"

She laughed at the thought. "I think she's afraid I'll serve them something weird."

"So you're not a horse person like your father?"

"I love horses. They're beautiful animals, but there's a difference between having horses for business and enjoyment. A few of our friends couldn't imagine having access to horses you never rode."

"You don't ride?" Wendell found her comment curious. He'd ridden since he was a young boy. He accepted the cup of coffee and the *profiteroles au chocolat*, pastry with vanilla ice cream and hot chocolate sauce, from the server.

"We rode in our limited spare time. We had chores around the home and the farm. Organized activities our parents planned to keep us out of trouble."

"Did you ever go to the races?" She shook her head and he asked, "Never?" His world revolved around the industry.

"My dad has very strong feelings about gambling."

"Didn't your sister win the lottery?"

"Yes, but she didn't buy the ticket."

"So how does one come by a winning lottery ticket without making a purchase?"

"One's boss gives it to them as a gift."

Wendell admired Ophelia's boldness as she mocked him. "Now that's an incredible gift."

"Actually Val considers it the answer to a prayer. She asked God to keep us at Sheridan Farm if it was His will."

He noted her reference to God. "You're a religious family?"

She nodded. "Very much so. I noticed the grand piano in the drawing room. Do you play?"

He inclined his head. "I do. My father said my mother said I would play the piano."

"How did she know?"

"Like you, my favorite toys were tiny pianos. Evidently, I banged on them enough to make her believe I had talent. I started lessons when I was very young. I surprised them by learning quickly."

"Would you play for me?"

He stood, offered his hand, and escorted her into the drawing room. "What would you like to hear?"

"You decide."

Wendell opted for Beethoven's "Moonlight Sonata." When he noted her rapt expression, he played through all three movements.

"That was beautiful," she said. Ophelia discreetly wiped away the tears. She brushed her hands up and down her arms. "You gave me chills. See."

He smiled and inclined his head.

"Have you ever played professionally?"

Wendell left the bench and took the chair across from her. "A time or two. Now I play for my friends and guests."

"You have an incredible gift."

He tilted his head again. "I'm honored."

"No. You're much too talented to play just for fun," she persisted. "You should use that talent to accomplish great things."

"Great things?" he repeated. After their earlier conversation, Wendell knew she would share her opinion soon enough.

"Yes. The world deserves to hear more of Wendell Hunter."

"You can tell that from one piece of music?"

"I appreciate beautiful music and those who make it happen. Yours is the type of talent that steals one's breath away."

"I wouldn't go that far."

"I would."

Wendell smiled. "You flatter me."

"You could play on any stage in the world. Why are you here in Kentucky?"

"It's where I belong."

All the time he'd worked toward a degree in music and trained with the best, Wendell's longing to know his father far exceeded his drive and ambition when it came to becoming a concert pianist. "In music, you perform or teach. I didn't care to do either on a professional level.

"So I returned home after college. Dad was spending

more time on the farm, and the opportunity to get to know him warred with my music. I chose home."

"You could have done concerts and spent time with him."

"Not quality time. I learned more about my father in the last few years of his life than I did in all the years past. I wouldn't exchange that time for any amount of fame."

The grandfather clock in the entry hall gonged the hour. "It's getting late," she said. "I should go. I'm sure your staff would like to call it a night."

Wendell stood and took her hand in his. Their gazes met and held. "I meant what I said, Ophelia. I don't regret tonight. It's been my pleasure."

"Mine, too."

"Even though you don't understand me?"

"I have a better idea of who you are," she said softly. "I suspect you share qualities with my dad. He's a man who values family above all else. You're searching for a woman who feels the same as you."

Her conclusion was right on target. "Do you value family, Ophelia?"

She nodded. "Every member of my family is precious to me. I depend on them to be there for me, and I do the same for them. There's nothing they could ask that I wouldn't do for them."

"What if they asked you to do something you considered to be wrong?"

"They'd never do that."

"How do you know?"

She winked at him. "Remember the parents who taught me right from wrong? That included not getting your brothers and sisters into trouble."

"They ruled with a firm hand?"

"Most definitely. With seven kids, they had to. Good night, Wendell. Thank you for a wonderful evening."

He walked her out to her car and opened the door for her. "Thank you for a very pleasurable experience, Ophelia. Drive safely."

three

Two nights later, Opie found herself dining in the presence of the other Hunter brother. She did comparisons between the two and found them to be very different.

That day, she'd considered her options while spending time with Jane's daughter, Sammy. When Jane took the job as Val's assistant, their mother suggested she bring her two-year-old to the farm every day. The little girl held a special place in the entire family's heart. When the child went down for her afternoon nap, Opie helped her mother prepare their evening meal. As usual, she lost the debate over trying something different with the ham.

A confrontation with a visitor brought her father in early. While Opie watched over dinner, her mother and Val calmed him down.

Later she learned Val's former coworker caused the uproar that upset their dad, blaming Val for losing his job and making threats. Opie hadn't been overly excited to hear they were thinking of hiring security but supposed it made sense to protect the family. As long as it didn't limit her freedom.

Thrilled over his new plans for her project, Val invited Russ to dinner to show the family what he'd done. She seated him next to their dad. Opie took her regular chair next to Val, and the noise died down when their father blessed the food.

As they passed bowls, Val introduced the family to Russ. When the conversation turned to the plans, Opie decided to speak up. "What do you think about me converting one of the outbuildings into a restaurant? I'd need to get financing, but I think it could work."

Val exchanged looks with their parents. "Are you sure? I thought you wanted to expand your horizons."

She'd considered where her degree could take her but found she enjoyed being home with her family. "I want to cook," she said. "And I've pretty much decided that I can be happier here than off somewhere missing all of you."

Val smiled. "We could find a restaurant in Lexington or Paris for that matter. Financing won't be as difficult as you fear. I've set aside monetary gifts for all three graduates."

"No, Val," Opie said without hesitation. "You've done enough."

Her sister grimaced playfully. "I have to give you something, and you can use the money to get what you want."

"It's a loan, Val. I intend to repay every dime," Opie declared. How would she prove herself if she leaned on her sister?

"Not your graduation gift."

"You're so stubborn."

"Wonder where I get it from," Val countered with a grin.

"All of you get it from your father," their mother teased, smiling at her husband.

"Hey now," their father exclaimed in mock affront. "In my family, it's called determination."

After the laughter died down, Opie said, "I could offer catering services to Your Wedding Place clientele."

"Won't that be too much?"

"Not if I hire sufficient staff. They should be able to work out of my restaurant kitchens."

Val said they'd discuss the catering later but expressed her concern that Opie would be much too busy once she opened a restaurant.

Russ caught her attention when he volunteered that there would be a commercial kitchen area in the structure's lower floor that could be used for catering. She definitely liked the idea of having access to a commercial kitchen.

The brainstorming session ended late. While Opie finished up in the kitchen, Val walked Russ out to his car. Opie noted a change in their attitudes toward each other tonight. Obviously, Russ redeemed himself with the new plans. When she checked the dining room one last time, she heard Val and her dad talking in the living room and paused when she heard her name.

"What about Opie's idea?" Val asked. "You think she could make it work?"

"I don't doubt any of my children can do anything they put their minds to. Opie's been a little flighty over the years, but cooking is the one thing she's stuck with. And she's good."

"I can see the benefit of having her here. In fact, I'd be willing to finance her restaurant."

"I don't think she wants you to do that," Jacob said.

She didn't. Opie went to their bedroom, grabbed her robe, and stomped into the bathroom. This family made it difficult to shine in a sky of stars. While the others knew what they wanted and worked hard to achieve it, she'd searched for herself. Now that her direction for the future was fixed, they doubted she could carry through. Opie knew exactly when she'd acquired the reputation for flightiness.

She couldn't blame anyone else for her father's opinion of her. Back when she'd been sixteen and working at the restaurant, she'd considered dropping out of high school. Her dad said she'd go if he had to sit in the chair next to hers all day. Eventually she lost her fascination with the dead-end job. Opie knew the only way she'd ever be able to do what she wanted was to have her own kitchen. She changed her focus and got her degree from culinary school.

Wrapped in her robe with a towel about her head, Opie sat on the bed polishing her toenails. Their younger sister, Jules, talked to a friend on the phone. Opie glanced up when Val entered the shared bedroom and asked, "Russ get off okay?"

"Why wouldn't he?" Val asked.

"I thought maybe his head had exploded from all those questions Jules asked," Opie remarked, dodging the stuffed animal their younger sister threw at her. "He had a distinct deer-in-the-headlights look a few times there when all of us got started."

Jules grabbed her robe and headed for the shower, leaving them alone.

"I think it came closer to bursting when I told him you went out with Wendell." Val dropped down on her bed. "He accused me of trying to interfere in their relationship."

Why had Val bought the date? She wouldn't mind knowing the answer to that one herself. Personally, Opie thought there was more to it than providing her an opportunity to get on her soapbox. She finished her toes and placed the polish on the nightstand. "What did you say to that?"

"That it had nothing to do with him."

Opie removed the towel and fluffed the damp tendrils. "Russ gets along well with the family, don't you think?"

Val refused to bite. "If you're so determined to play matchmaker, why don't you work on Heath and Jane?"

"Is that why you made her your assistant?"

"She needed the job, and I know she'll be an asset. She has a lot of managerial experience. Just wait. You'll see how good she is."

Opie shoved a pillow behind her back and propped against the headboard. "Have you seen how Heath looks at her?"

"I think he's always had a crush on Jane but decided she was out of his league."

"And now she's going to be working here all day while he's landscaping your project."

"I don't know about that, Opie," Val said, expressing her concern. "I can't reconcile him spending years in college to come home and landscape."

"You heard what Mom said. It's Heath's choice."

"But is he doing it for the right reason?"

"You told Rom he had time when he went for the interview. Why not offer Heath the same option?"

"I'll talk to him," Val said. "Is this restaurant what you want to do?"

Opie shrugged. "Ideas are bouncing around in my head faster than I can process. Even more since Russ mentioned expanding the kitchen in the structure. I could run a catering business from there."

"You just like the idea of having a commercial kitchen at your disposal," Val teased.

"Every chef's dream," Opie agreed.

"Nothing has to be decided right away."

Opie pumped lotion into her hand and smoothed it over her arms and legs. "Russ really redeemed himself with that plan today, didn't he?"

"Yes," Val said. "I couldn't believe you said what you did."

She made a major faux pas when she commented that the plans had come a long way. Opie grinned and said, "Sorry. It slipped out. I tried to backpedal."

Val giggled. "We noticed." She hesitated. "Opie, what do you think about moving into the Sheridans' house?"

Definitely an idea she could appreciate. "Having my own bedroom? Sign me up."

"Daddy and I are praying over the situation. Will you pray, too?" Opie nodded and Val continued. "There's something else. I feel God is directing me to visit Grandfather Truelove."

"I doubt Daddy would jump on board with that."

"Daddy has to forgive Grandfather. I think God wants us to help him find peace."

"I'll add that to my prayer list," she promised.

&

Thoughts of Ophelia's ambush stayed with Wendell. Though he hadn't told her, he found it interesting that her career choice reflected largely in a traditional homemaker's role. He knew she'd come to that realization as she matured.

He considered the points she'd made and wondered if she was right. Did the woman he sought exist? Or had he made choices that would keep him searching forever? Still, he did plan to choose carefully and fully commit when he found her.

With the obligation of the date behind him, Wendell returned to business as usual. He scheduled a meeting to discuss Dell Air's future with his trainer that afternoon.

The horse's name always made him chuckle. Two years before, his romantic interest at the time wanted to name the new foal. They were in the office, and she'd been looking over the sheet of stud fees for the various stallions on the farm. "You should name this one Dell Air. You know, like Bel Air. He's pretty exclusive, too."

He submitted the name to the Jockey Club for approval, and it was accepted. The colt did well in his maiden race, and Wendell hadn't minded having his name associated with a winner. He felt optimistic that the progeny of his father's Triple Crown stallion might help him break free of the losing streak he'd been on since his father's death.

Mrs. Carroll tapped on his office door. "Sorry to disturb you, Mr. Hunter, but we have a situation."

His executive housekeeper immediately captured his attention. They rarely had situations. His home ran so smoothly that he'd come to expect things with very little regard as to how they happened. He supposed that attitude did sound a bit feudal. Ophelia's admonishment about taking his employees for granted came to mind.

"Jean-Pierre has been called home due to family sickness. He would like to fly out tonight if possible."

"His grandmother?" Wendell knew the elderly woman wasn't in the best of health.

She nodded, her solemn expression telling him the news wasn't good.

"What does the schedule look like?" Wendell didn't mind fending for himself, but he'd hired a chef to provide his guests with the best.

"Your next guests come closer to the end of June."

"Will he be back by then?"

"He doesn't know. He did say his grandmother is very ill."

Wendell knew how he'd felt about his own grandmother. Nothing would have kept him from her in her time of need. "Tell him to make his plans. We'll find a temporary replacement."

"I'll inform Jean-Pierre."

"Mrs. Carroll," he called when she started from the room. "Please tell Jean-Pierre I'm thinking of them both."

After she'd gone, Wendell thumbed through the Rolodex, looking for the number of the Lexington employment agency.

❧

No matter how she tried, Opie found it impossible to get Wendell Hunter off her mind. One evening had given her a better understanding, but Opie knew unraveling the man's complexity would take a lifetime. She'd only seen the glimpses that he'd allowed her to see. She would have liked to see more.

He and Russ were very different. She wondered what could have caused the incident that tore them apart.

Losing his mother so young must have been very difficult for a small boy. Opie could see how that would make it even more imperative that he proceed cautiously in his search for his soul mate. And even if she didn't care for his requirements for a wife, she liked that he was committed to finding a woman and making a home for his family. So many men seemed not to care about settling down.

She heard the phone ring and her mother's voice. "Opie, phone."

Pushing aside her second cup of coffee, she rose and picked up the cordless from the counter. "Hi, Opie. It's Sarah Beth." They caught up for a few minutes before the young woman asked, "Are you looking for work?"

Opie supposed she was looking in a roundabout way. Or at least she would be once she made up her mind about the future. "I should be."

"Someone there in Paris needs a chef for a limited time."

She stood straighter.

"They want extensive training in various cuisines and cooking skills," Sarah Beth said. "Team environment, respect for other's property, discretion, good work ethics," she read as by rote. "Duties include preparing up to three meals per day along with organizing food orders. They want references and plan to do a background check." She chuckled and said, "Of course that's not an issue for you."

This job sounded custom-made for her, Opie thought.

"Where do I apply?"

"They said to fax resumes to Hunter Farm." She recited the number.

What had happened to Wendell's chef? Limited time meant he hadn't resigned. Whatever the case, this was the perfect opportunity to tell Wendell about her personal chef services.

"So are you interested? Mom says it's okay if the two of you work out a mutually beneficial deal."

Opie was confused. Elizabeth King ran a staffing agency. "But what about the placement fee?"

"She's not worried about that. Your parents have helped us more than once over the years. She says we can repay the favor and not disappoint Mr. Hunter at the same time. She gets a lot of business from him and his friends. So can I tell her you'll follow up with him?"

"Yes, I'll get in touch with Wendell Hunter right away. Thanks, Sarah Beth. And thank your mom for thinking of me."

For Opie, *right away* meant now. She didn't intend to let this possibility slip between her fingers. She opted for a surprise attack.

After changing into a soft plum summer suit, Opie applied a bit of lipstick. She then placed her current résumé into a presentation folder and slipped it into the briefcase she'd received from her parents for graduation.

Taking keys from the rack by the door, Opie told her mother where she was going. She formulated what she would say to Wendell during the drive to Hunter Farm.

After giving her name, Opie waited in the entry hall until the woman returned to escort her to his office. Wendell rose from behind his desk when she entered. Today he wore jeans as easily as he'd worn the tuxedo. "Ophelia, come in," he greeted. "What a pleasant surprise. What can I do for you?"

"I'm your woman."

Wendell looked taken aback.

"For the job," she tacked on hurriedly. "The agency gave me a call. I know you said to fax a résumé, but I had an idea I wanted to propose."

He came around the desk and indicated she should have a seat on the sofa. He chose a leather wingback chair for himself and asked, "What did you have in mind?"

She immediately jumped into the speech she'd rehearsed. "I thought you might consider the services of a personal chef. You wouldn't have to pay a full-time person. I could come into your kitchen and prepare food on a per meal basis. Think of it as on-site catering."

"Did you bring the résumé?"

Hoping to wow him with her qualifications and accomplishments, Opie pulled the folder from her case and handed it over.

He reviewed the information and glanced at her. "May I consider your proposal and get back to you?"

Opie nodded. "Certainly. I'd love the opportunity to demonstrate my skills. I don't think you'd be disappointed."

"What is your specialty?"

"American regional cuisine. Though I am capable of a wide variety of dishes."

"I'll let you know," Wendell said. "Would you care to join me for a cool drink before you go?"

She agreed, and he called the kitchen to request lemonade.

≥∂

Wendell noted that she'd made herself completely at home. She'd kicked off her shoes and sat with her legs curled underneath her just as his mother had done in the portriat over the sofa. Meredith Steele Hunter had also been a petite blond. Probably close to Ophelia's age when she married his father.

His dad said his mother loved to curl up on the sofa while he worked. Maybe that was why his father hadn't allowed Nicole to replace the black leather couch. He'd claimed to like the room as it was.

Wendell did, too. After their deaths, he'd been tempted to rid the house of Nicole's decorating choices, but he'd only done a judicious editing for Russ's sake. When he considered Russ hadn't set foot in the house since his furtive weekend departure, he wondered why he bothered.

Russ removed items listed as his in the will and left a childish I-hate-you letter. Wendell attempted to contact him, but Russ refused to take his calls and changed his numbers. The attorney contacted Russ to no avail. Wendell tired of the games and decided Russ would be the one to initiate any future communication.

Wendell found his gaze shifting from Ophelia to the painting, searching for similarities. There were few beyond hair and eye color. And the way she sat.

He'd found the portrait in the attic along with boxes of photos from his childhood. Other items that Nicole must have decided were better out of sight reposed there as well. Wendell returned the painting to its rightful place in this room. Then he placed the other items where he could enjoy them.

Over the years, Nicole made a point of focusing on her husband and son and pushing anything to do with Wendell and his mother deep into the recesses of her husband's mind. Wendell didn't know whom he resented more—his dad for allowing it or Nicole for treating him that way.

Throughout his childhood, the only photos downstairs were of his dad and Nicole with a tiny photo of him with Russ on their father's desk. Portraits of mother and son, namely Nicole and Russ, had been prominent in the master suite.

Wendell personally removed those items to the bedroom that had been Russ's since birth. Maybe one day he'd pass them on to his half brother. Or follow Nicole's example and banish them to the attic when he married and started his own family. Whatever the case, her efforts to push him out of his father's life to benefit her son had been wasted when the will indicated Russ was not entitled to one inch of Hunter Farm. Wendell derived more enjoyment from Nicole's failure than his fractured relationship with his brother.

"Wendell? Did you hear me?"

He looked up. "Sorry. What were you saying?"

"You were a million miles away. I asked what happened to Jean-Pierre."

"He had a family emergency in Paris."

"Oh, I'm sorry. I hope everything is okay."

He nodded. "He called Mrs. Carroll to say his grand-mother is improving."

"Good. Russ came to dinner at our place Thursday night."

How could she possibly know he'd been thinking of Russ? "How is he?"

Wendell knew exactly how his half brother was doing. They might not get along, but, out of respect to their father, he did what he could to help his younger brother.

"Val wasn't impressed by his first efforts, but he did a complete 360 on the new idea."

Her slip of the tongue caught Wendell's attention. Back when Russ graduated and went looking for a job, Wendell phoned Randall King and requested a favor. Russ didn't know, and Wendell did not intend to tell him what he'd done. He'd spoken to Randall a couple of times since and learned he was satisfied with Russ's work.

Ophelia gasped, covering her mouth with her hands as she said, "I shouldn't have told you that."

In his brother's defense, Wendell knew creating plans was no easy task. He recalled the work they put in with their architect when they added the new barn a few years back. They sent the man back to the drawing table several times.

"I promise not to tell him." Wendell didn't add that it would be impossible since he never saw Russ. "I take it these plans are close to completion. Can you tell me anything more?"

"I suppose I could say she plans to operate a wedding venue business at Sheridan Farm."

Wendell didn't understand. "Wedding venue? On a horse farm?"

"Why not? It's a beautiful area."

He frowned and said, "I'm not disputing that, but it's a working horse farm."

"You're sounding like your brother."

Perhaps they still shared similar feelings on the things that truly mattered. "Russ didn't agree with the project?"

"He put aside his reservations for the sake of his job."

"Do you mean she's not going to operate the farm any longer?"

"I never said any such thing," she exclaimed in irritation. "Why would you think that?"

"You said a wedding business," Wendell said, thinking he'd never heard anything so stupid in his life.

"Only on a minimal portion of the acreage. Daddy will run the farm while Val runs Your Wedding Place."

"Your Wedding Place?"

"That's the name of her business."

"And what is it you say she's providing? Venues?"

"I've already said more than I should." Ophelia shut up tighter than a clam.

"I'm sorry," he offered, hoping to appease her. "I'm curious about what's going on in the neighborhood."

"I'll tell Val you have concerns."

"I'm sure she's aware that others will take issue with changes affecting our lifestyles," Wendell offered, trying not to antagonize her even more.

"She's as entitled to her business as you are."

"She is," he agreed, "but there are considerations to this type of business. That's why I asked about your plans for a restaurant at the farm. Increasing the traffic in this area will destroy the easy lifestyle we all enjoy."

"Everything will be handled properly. Val is sensitive to the needs of others and won't do anything to harm the community. She loves it as much as you do."

She might not plan to change things, but Wendell knew the best-laid plans often went awry. "How does your father feel about her plans?"

"He supports Val." Her gaze shifted to the far wall and the small portrait hanging there. "That horse reminds me of Fancy. Daddy says she has the potential to produce a winner. He claims she's got a bit of gazelle in her when she runs."

"She's that fast?"

She nodded. "Daddy says she runs like the wind."

The horse in the portrait was Merri's Girl. She'd been his father's wedding gift to his mother when they married thirty-three years before. Could this Fancy somehow be related to his mother's mare? "How did your dad acquire his horse?"

"She's a four-year-old filly. Daddy attended a sale with Mr. Sheridan. From the moment he laid eyes on her, he insisted she showed great potential. Mom always said she'd be jealous if Fancy wasn't a horse," Ophelia offered with a little laugh. "Anyway, Mr. Sheridan bought her and named her Jacob's Fancy. He left her to Daddy."

"You say she looks like the horse in the picture?"

Ophelia nodded. A wave of nostalgia washed over him. Merri's Girl died when Wendell was eighteen years old. Both he and his dad stood by when they laid her heart, hooves, and head to rest on the farm. Her death severed yet another link with his mother.

"So what do you think?"

Her question confused him. "About the horse?"

"No," she said. "Do you think we could work together? I'm an excellent chef. I think you'd find having a personal chef easier than hiring a stranger to fill a temporary position." She leaned forward and asked, "What's your favorite meal? I'd love to cook for you and show you how good I am."

Wendell remained noncommittal. He wasn't about to agree to anything before giving it a great deal of thought. His experience with Ophelia Truelove guaranteed she'd shake up his home and probably his life if he said yes. "There's no need for that. I'm sure your references will speak for themselves. I'll look over your résumé and let you know."

She finished her lemonade and set the glass on the tray. "I should let you get back to work. Thanks for your time."

❧

Wendell decided to visit Jacob Truelove with a proposition of his own. It took one look at the filly they called Jacob's Fancy to know she came from Hunter Farm. The beautiful bay stood sixteen hands high and was a chestnut color with three white socks.

Wendell remembered the filly. She'd been the produce of Stryker Heart, Merri's Girl's daughter. His dad insisted on selling the foal. Wendell hadn't known who bought her, hadn't wanted to know for fear he might try to buy her back. For as long as he could remember, his father insisted he not become attached to the horses. "Ophelia's right. She does look like Merri's Girl. Your Fancy came from Hunter Farm."

"She did." Jacob named her dam.

"Ophelia says that you think she has potential."

Jacob nodded. "I worked with her and the trainer. Watching her run gave me this gut feeling that she has potential for greatness."

"I don't suppose Dad saw her in the same way. He always said you couldn't keep every animal that comes across your farm."

"I knew Mr. Sheridan could sell her at any time, but I think he realized how attached I'd become and decided to give her to me."

Wendell wondered if his father would have made a winner of the filly if she'd stayed at Hunter Farm. "So Mr. Sheridan raced her?"

"He did. She managed a fair number of first, second, and third place finishes until she injured her leg."

"What makes you feel as you do?"

"I've seen enough champion horseflesh to know. Fancy has an incredible spirit."

"How will the leg affect her as a brood mare?"

"She'll be okay," Jacob said confidently. "She's tough, my Fancy."

Wendell remembered what Ophelia said about her father's relationship with the horse. "I have Thrill Hunter at the farm. What if we cover her and see what happens?"

Jacob Truelove hesitated. "That stallion has a steep stud fee."

"I could waive the fee if you're willing to make a deal. If the foal is a colt, I get it and we cover your Fancy a second time.

If it's a filly, you keep it and pay stud fees for future dealings."

"You make it hard to say no."

"Then don't." Wendell reached out his hand. After a slight hesitation, Jacob Truelove shook on the deal. "Ophelia mentioned her sister's plans to run a business from the farm." From his closed expression, Wendell could see Jacob wasn't going to tell him anything either.

"She shouldn't have said anything."

"She didn't say a lot. Just enough to give me concerns about the influence on the neighborhood. What's your thought?"

"There will be spurts of activity, but I don't think it will be unmanageable. Val has your brother working up plans, and I'm sure they're taking everything into consideration."

"So you're okay with her converting the farm for her business?"

"Don't see how I can complain. It's hers to do as she pleases."

"Why wouldn't she want to keep Sheridan Farm as is?"

"The farm won't change. Val gave it to her mother and me. This other business is her dream. I can understand that she'd want to carry through now that she has means to do so."

Wendell doubted things would go as smoothly as they thought. "I hope it doesn't cause problems."

"Val will do everything possible to make it work for everyone. That's the kind of person she is."

"That's what Ophelia said. I'll be in touch with you to finalize the arrangements."

Jacob nodded. "I'll look forward to hearing from you."

❧

"Did he come to see me?" Opie asked over lunch when her father mentioned Wendell Hunter's visit.

"No. He came to see me about a horse. And to express his concern about your business," he told Val.

She stopped eating and asked, "What does he know about my business?"

"You'll have to ask your sister."

Opie swallowed hard. "I'm sorry, Val. I thought it would

be okay to say you planned to open a wedding venue business. I didn't say any more after it became obvious he didn't like the idea. When he started asking questions, I told him I'd tell you he's concerned about the increased traffic flow."

"And when did you plan to tell me?"

"When the time was right?" She grimaced. "I'm really sorry. Guess I was nervous or something. We were talking, and it slipped out."

Val's spluttered laughter burst forth with abandon. "Nervous? You? I'd think he would be the nervous one once you got started. Mom said you went to talk to him about a job. How did it go?"

"He's thinking it over. Probably thinks I'm too young. It's just as well. Lulu called this morning. She offered to pay my airfare to New York if I'd come up to help her. Said we'd go to the food show."

"So now you understand why I asked everyone to keep the business information quiet?"

"Yes. I should have realized he'd go overboard." Opie glanced at her dad. "You say he came to see you about a horse?" She couldn't imagine they had anything Wendell considered worthy of his stables. Val negotiated the sale to retain a few of the Sheridan's more expensive stallions, and her dad planned to buy more, but it would take time for them to reach Hunter Farm's standards.

"He's offered to cover Fancy free of charge." Their dad went on to outline the plan.

"Sounds like he's getting the better end of the deal," Opie offered.

"Equal possibility the foal will be female," her dad said. "And if not, there's always the second time. Any way you look at it, I get a quality horse out of the deal."

"Yeah, but that's two years away if it's a colt."

"Doesn't matter. Fancy came from Hunter Farm. She holds a special place in Wendell's heart."

Opie supposed that with his love of the farm he would

share equal regard for the animals that supported his liveli-hood. Still she found the idea that he felt a sentimental attach-ment to a horse surprising. "Why would you think that?"

"I could see it in his expression when he looked at her. Her dam came from his mother's horse."

"He sure didn't lose any time getting over here to check her out. I saw a portrait at his home and mentioned the horse reminded me of Fancy."

Her dad shook his head in amazement. "Free stud fees to a Derby winner. I can't reject that kind of deal."

four

"May I speak to Ophelia?"

After giving the matter a great deal of consideration, Wendell concluded he had nothing to lose by accepting Ophelia's proposal. Her references were very complimentary and assured him she was an excellent cook. He looked forward to learning what comprised American Regional Cuisine.

"Opie's not here."

"Do you know when she'll be home?" he asked, thinking she was out running errands.

"Next week. She's in New York."

That surprised him. "I just returned from Belmont and wanted to talk to her about the job I have."

"Did she give you her cell number?"

He rifled through the papers on his desktop and pulled out her résumé folder. "Yes. It's here on the business card."

"You should call her. I'm sure she wouldn't mind."

"I will. Thanks."

"Wendell?"

He paused as Val Truelove called his name just before he disconnected. "Yes?"

"Did you have a horse running in the Stakes?"

Wendell wondered why she'd asked. "Not this year. Thanks for your help. Have a good day."

There were similar inquiries from his father's friends. His gaze shifted to the glass case. The numerous trophies were a testament to his father's ability to choose winning horses. Wendell knew people expected him to assume his father's role. At present, his breeding program prospered because of his father's winning stallions, but that would only last so long. His own Triple Crown hope for this year died the week before the Preakness.

He dialed Ophelia's cell number. She called hello among the cacophony of kitchen sounds.

"Hi. It's Wendell Hunter."

"Wendell?" She sounded far away.

"Hope you don't mind me calling you there. Your sister told me you were in New York."

"No. Not at all."

"I wanted to talk about your proposal."

The clatter was almost deafening.

"Let me get out of this kitchen so I can hear you." The noise volume lessened. "There that's better," she said shortly. "Kitchens are always controlled chaos. Now what did you want to discuss?"

"Your proposal. I have important guests arriving in two weeks. Jean-Pierre is not going to be back, and I wanted to engage you as my personal chef while they're in-house. I'll need three meals a day for the majority of the time though there are a few days they will only be around for dinner. Are you willing to work around their schedules?"

"Of course. When would you like to discuss menus?"

Other than special requests now and then, Wendell left the menu planning to his staff. "Why don't you prepare those?"

"Do your guests have food preferences? Any allergies?"

"I have no idea." He wined and dined buyers and breeders on a regular basis, hoping to make a favorable impression with his horses and hospitality. And he depended on his staff to keep him apprised of who was expected and when.

"Where are they from?"

Wendell didn't have the answers. "I pay Jean-Pierre to handle those details."

"I can prepare the food, but I'll need to know what to prepare," she insisted.

He hired people to deal with the minutiae, leaving him free to deal with the more important things demanding his attention. "Check with Mrs. Carroll. Give her your lists, and she'll see to it that your orders are placed."

"I prefer doing some of my shopping," Opie said. "The

farmer's market has such wonderful fresh produce this time of year."

"That's fine. Once we come to an agreement, I'll expect you to handle everything. I'll draw up the contract for your signature. When will you be back?"

"When do you need me?"

"Next week."

"I'll be there."

Wendell hoped Ophelia wouldn't let him down. Her decision to go to New York after the interview bothered him. But as promised, she arrived home at the first of the week and contacted Mrs. Carroll right away. She came to see him to sign the agreement he'd drawn up.

"Mrs. Carroll says your guests are Americans. That makes my job easier."

"Sorry I couldn't answer that for you." He'd just received the list that morning in an e-mail. "Did you enjoy your trip to New York?"

"I stayed busy. A friend asked me to help at her restaurant, and I attended a food show. Val said you were in New York. Did you have a horse running in the Belmont Stakes?"

Why were the Truelove women so interested in his horses? "No. I haven't had a run of good luck with my horses since my father's death. He always had horses in the Triple Crown races."

"Don't you own the same horses?"

"I've retired some recently. They're standing stud. A couple more were euthanized after severe injuries. I'm always on the lookout for that next winner. I know they're out there."

"They are. Daddy raises beautiful horses."

"But he doesn't race them?"

"No. He breeds quality stock and works with the trainers. He loves to watch them on the track at the farm."

"Why bother?"

"There's nothing more beautiful than a Thoroughbred stretched out in a full run, his shiny coat and muscles flexing in the joy of the moment. Their pleasure in running far exceeds the thrill of money wins."

Wendell agreed but found it difficult to reconcile one with the other. "I'd ask how he plans to support the farm if he's not planning to race, but I already know." No doubt, his daughter would pay out a substantial portion of her winnings to keep the farm afloat.

"Daddy plans to make the farm self-supporting. He will breed and sell horses. He can claim a champion just as easily from the breeding standpoint as the racing. He'll also board animals."

"William Sheridan raced his horses."

"Daddy managed the farm, but he never dealt with that side of the business. Mr. Sheridan was satisfied to leave the farm in his hands and let the trainers and jockeys handle the races."

"Why does your father object to racing?"

"It's not the racing," Opie said. "It's the gambling."

"Does he have a problem?" Wendell had never heard any gossip about Jacob Truelove in the horse circles but supposed it could be the case.

"Daddy?" Opie asked, sounding incredulous. "The man who questioned his daughter accepting the proceeds of a lottery ticket her boss gifted her? You think he has a problem?"

"Well no, but generally people who are that antigambling either have a problem or have family members. . ."

Wendell trailed off. He never understood how his conversations with Ophelia kept going until he got himself in too deep to get out.

"My grandfather Truelove has a problem. Gambling is not something we do in the Truelove home."

Wendell paid a great deal of attention to stacking the papers she handed him. "I'm sorry. I didn't know." He ran the pages through the copier and handed her a set. He had to ask the next question. "What happened to your grandfather?"

"Daddy's entire family suffered because he refused to change his behavior. My grandmother nearly died of a heart attack. Daddy had a difficult life but taught us that God would take care of us if we trusted in Him."

A red flag went up in Wendell's head. She hadn't been as

open to the conversation as usual. Perhaps he'd been too personal on a topic she didn't care to discuss.

"That doesn't work for me, Ophelia. If there is a God, He took my mother and then my father when I finally had a chance to know him. And my brother."

"You still have Russ," she protested.

"He wants nothing to do with me. We haven't spoken to each other since I inherited the farm. It's all about luck, Ophelia. I'll find the horse that makes it happen for me and when I do, you'll see God has nothing to do with it."

"That's not true! God has everything to do with our lives. Whether you believe that or not, God is in control."

❧

Opie met her dad in the yard when coming out of the house. "Will you give this to Wendell?" he asked. "It's Fancy's daybook. I thought he might like to take a look."

She tucked it into her big purse and climbed into the waiting SUV. Upon her arrival, Opie checked in with Mrs. Carroll and mentioned that she needed to drop off something to Wendell. After their last conversation, she expected the situation between them to be tense.

"Daddy thought you might like to see this."

She noted his interest as he thumbed through the pages. "Tell him thanks. I'll get it back to him soon."

"I'm finalizing the plans today," Opie said. "Anything special you'd care to see included?"

"I'm a big fan of desserts."

She smiled. "I'll see what I can do."

"Ophelia," he called when she started from the room. She paused, wondering if he would bring up the exchange. "Did something happen over at your place? I noticed the security vehicles by the gate."

"You mean our own little secret service?" Opie didn't care for the restrictions placed on them by the new security firm. Used to going where she wanted when she wanted, she didn't like having to ask someone to drive her. "The women in our family are no longer allowed to travel without escort. Security brought me over and will pick me up when I call to say I'm ready. I'm surprised they don't stand guard outside."

"What happened?"

"A disgruntled former coworker of Val's showed up at the farm. I never imagined her winning the money would make us prisoners in our own home. Daddy wants Val to hire a bodyguard. Can you imagine? And he said she needs to get a better car."

"She doesn't like the idea?"

"She did say it would look silly to have a driver with the old car she has now." Opie giggled at the thought. "Mom thinks it's a small price to pay for the blessings we've been given."

"There are a lot of bad things going on in the world, Ophelia. It makes sense to watch your back until you see how things go. I can't say people will ever forget anyone winning that kind of money."

"It does give people ideas. Val's convinced that anyone who wanted to get to her would go through us to do so. I know she has a point. Doesn't mean I have to like it, though. Gotta run. Mrs. Carroll is waiting on me."

⚜

Wendell didn't understand the need for overkill. He'd lived in their peaceful community for years and never considered a need for security. Of course, he wasn't a woman. Perhaps Jacob had a point. Fear for a wife or child could change his mind.

As a single man with no one they could use to get to him, Wendell didn't present a similar problem. He couldn't even name a person who would pay his ransom. Certainly not Russ.

Growing up, his dad warned him to be cautious. He stayed out of the places where he could get into trouble. Even in college, when his friends visited bars in the worst sections of town, he refused to go. He'd witnessed the battered faces his friends sported after a night of drinking with a rough crowd.

When they kept going back for more, Wendell decided they liked to fight.

He'd hate to see anything happen to Ophelia or any of her family. While it didn't seem fair to curtail her travel, it was prudent of them to think ahead.

five

How could two weeks pass so quickly? Opie wondered as she prepared for her final service. Tonight Wendell invited several of his Paris friends to join him and his guests for dinner. She'd reworked the menu after Mrs. Carroll phoned to tell her.

"Is there anyone who could help in the kitchen?" Opie knew she'd need another set of hands with more people to feed.

"I'll ask Mr. Wendell."

"If not, I can ask my family."

Mrs. Carroll called back to say that one of the staff would help. Opie liked the young woman who introduced herself as April. She gave her a list of tasks and started work on her own list.

"Is this what you want?" April asked, showing Opie the pile of red bell peppers.

"Chop them a bit finer," Opie said, taking the knife and demonstrating what she wanted. "And curl your fingers under. I don't need you chopping off anything important."

The young woman chuckled and went back to work.

"That's perfect," Opie said after looking on for a minute.

"I help Jean-Pierre at times. He calls me his *sous*-chef. Whatever that is."

"That means he's made you his second in command. Do you like to cook?"

"I like to eat Jean-Pierre's food."

"It is good," Opie agreed.

"That looks really good," April commented when Opie dipped soup into demitasse cups. "What is it?"

"Cucumber gazpacho."

When April's stomach growled, she grinned and said, "I missed lunch today."

"You shouldn't do that."

"Yes I should," April said. "I'm not blessed to be a tiny little thing like you."

Opie filled an extra cup and handed it to her. "Try this, and tell me what you think."

She put the others on a serving tray and sent the *amuse-bouche*, flavorful little bite, out to the guests.

"That was yummy," April exclaimed. "What's for dessert?"

"Didn't I hear something about not being blessed?"

"You wouldn't make a grown woman cry, would you?"

Opie chuckled. "I made three desserts for tonight. I'm sure we can find something to appeal to you."

"My mouth is watering already."

The menu consisted of a fresh mixed greens salad with Dijon vinaigrette, homemade yeast rolls, an entrée of beef tenderloin with blue cheese and herb crust, sautéed green beans, and roasted garlic mashed potatoes. Opie set aside samples of each for an appreciative April.

After plating the dessert choices of cheesecake with strawberries, tiny chocolate cakes, and lemon squares, she breathed a sigh of relief and sat down. "I think we're okay. No one sent anything back."

"Only empty plates. I'd say it was a successful party."

Opie smiled and said, "That's the only kind I like."

April yawned widely and apologized. "My baby woke me at five this morning. He's teething."

"Where is he now?"

"My mom keeps him while I work. My husband picks him up when he gets off."

Opie sent April home and attacked the cleanup on her own. Sometime later, she heard car doors slamming and knew the party was over.

She finished packing her knives and looked around the kitchen one last time to assure herself everything was in order. She'd enjoyed working for Wendell. The buyers, longtime acquaintances of the Sheridan family, were very appreciative of her efforts. Opie felt encouraged that more people in the area would welcome the services of a private chef. She just needed to promote herself.

"Good. You're still here," Wendell said as he hurried into the room. "I wanted to give you this."

She accepted the envelope. "I would have billed you."

"I wanted to tell you personally how much I've appreciated everything you've done. Mrs. Carroll says you've been a pleasure to work with."

Opie smiled. "I enjoyed working with her, too. You're fortunate to have such caring staff."

"They make my life easier. What will you do now?"

Her mind whirled with the possibilities. "I was just thinking about that. I've enjoyed working as a private chef, so I'll probably look for more work and maybe some catering on the side if I can find a kitchen. I'm in charge of the church's annual food drive, and then I'm cooking for Daddy's birthday party in August."

"Feel free to use me as a reference."

Pleasure filled her. Just maybe Wendell understood how important this was to her. "Thank you. Would you care for café mocha before I go?"

Each night after dinner, she'd prepared pots of the coffee-hot chocolate combination for the dinner guests. When Wendell said yes, she took down a pot from the overhead rack, removed milk from the fridge, and reached for the canister she'd left on the counter. She planned to leave the mixture as a thank-you gift for Wendell.

Opie turned on the stove, and there was a hesitation before the fire leaped up in the air. Surprised, she fell back, and Wendell grabbed her, swiftly turning off the stove before using his hands to beat out the flames that engulfed the sleeve of her white chef's jacket.

"Are you okay? Remove the jacket and let me check your arm," he demanded.

Dazed, Opie didn't protest when he reached for her buttons. She wore a white tee underneath. Together they examined her arm. There were one or two red spots. "What happened?"

"I have no idea," he said, pulling her over to place her arm under cold water from the faucet. "Has the stove given you any problems this week?"

"Not at all. It's been one of the better stoves I've used."

"I'll get a serviceman out here tomorrow. Are you okay?"

"A little surprised." Opie trembled beneath the hand resting on her shoulder.

"You need to calm down before you leave. I'll fix you a cold drink."

"I can. . ."

"No," Wendell said, his voice sounding strange. He handed her a towel. "Sit down. I can put ice and soda in a glass."

"It's not the first time I've been on fire, you know," Opie said as she watched him mop milk from the floor with a paper towel.

Wendell paused and stared at her. "Does this type of thing happen often in the kitchen?"

"There's always a safety consideration. Hot pots, handles, spoons, grease flare-ups, splashes. All part of the job."

"You could have been badly burned."

"But I wasn't," she countered. "I'm just a bit unnerved by the unexpectedness of the incident."

He filled two glasses with ice and took a bottle from the fridge. "Let's sit on the porch."

Opie followed and chose the swing looking out onto the Hunters' garden. Her gaze shifted from place to place with the nightscape lighting, and the sound of water caught her ear. "It's beautiful. Heath would love this area."

"Who is Heath?"

She recalled Wendell didn't know the rest of her family. "My brother. He and Rom, they're twins, graduated from Harvard last month. Rom took a job in Lexington. Heath is helping Val with the gardens while he considers his options."

"You all have nicknames?"

Opie explained that her mother loved the classics and gave them her favorite name at the time. "Val is Valentine, Heath is

Heathcliff, Rom is Romeo, Jules is Juliet, Roc is Rochester, and Cy is Darcy. Jules, Roc, and Cy are still in school. Jules plans to become an architect, and Cy wants to be a vet. Roc will probably do something in science."

"Impressive. Your parents must be proud."

"My dad's determined that none of his children will follow in his father's footsteps. He helped my uncle Zeb get his degree. He's a Harvard professor. Uncle Zeb helped my aunt Karen become a doctor. She lives near my grandmother in Florida and does cancer research. I stayed with her when I attended culinary school."

"How's your arm?"

Opie fingered the places that were only slightly sensitive. "I'm fine. Like I said, burns and cuts are everyday occurrences in the kitchen."

"Not in my kitchen."

"You should warn Jean-Pierre the stove is acting up." The chef planned to report back to work at the first of the week.

"I'll see to it that the situation is corrected first thing tomorrow."

Opie didn't doubt someone would be out immediately.

"I can't thank you enough, Ophelia. You've certainly impressed me. You're a wonderful chef."

She bloomed with the compliment. Hearing Wendell say it meant so much more.

"One of the men threatened to steal you away."

"You didn't tell him I'm the substitute?"

"A smart man never plays all his cards. I think they were most impressed when you managed to learn their favorites and prepare them. They said they don't generally get such a treat."

"I appreciate the opportunity. Mom is such a stickler for basic food that I don't experiment as often as I'd like."

"Why did you come back to Paris?"

"I missed my family."

Opie wondered if he considered that a silly reason not to strike out into new frontiers for the career she wanted so badly.

"Val won the money and started making plans for her business. She gifted me with money to finance my dream."

"And your dream is a restaurant at the farm?"

"I don't know," she admitted. "Restaurants entail a level of responsibility I don't know that I want to take on. I want to cook. Catering and private chef work appeals to me. Thanks to Val I can consider options I didn't have before."

"I'd like to help. Though I'm not fully convinced I'm doing you a favor. That fire incident tonight showed me how dangerous your work could be. But if you're determined to do this, I'll certainly refer you to my friends."

Opie barely noticed the sting of the burn. She'd done more damage in her student days. "You have a passion for horses. I have that same zeal for food. We take the risks associated with our respective careers as routine occurrences." She paused for a moment and added, "I'm thankful the stove didn't malfunction when I had meals to prepare and that I wasn't hurt any worse." A clock chimed the midnight hour in distant parts of the house. "It's getting late. I should get home."

When she stood, he did the same. She stretched out her hand to him. "Thanks again for the opportunity. Please keep me in mind for the future."

Wendell grimaced slightly when he took her hand.

"Are you okay?" she demanded, turning his hand over in hers. His reddened palm answered the question. "Why didn't you say something? You were hurt worse than me. Are they uncomfortable?"

"I'm fine."

"That's such a man answer," she disparaged, quickly taking control. "There's burn cream in the first-aid kit."

She held his hand and pulled him along into the kitchen. Mrs. Carroll had shown her the location of the kit and the fire extinguisher on her first day. Opie quickly found what she needed. Taking his hand in hers, she carefully massaged the cream into his palm. Aware of him, she paused and looked into his eyes. "I don't want to hurt you."

Wendell took over the task. "I suppose the ice in the glass masked the sting."

"I'm sorry."

"It was my stove that malfunctioned. My hands will be fine by the morning." She hesitated and Wendell said, "I should drive you home."

"I'll call for someone to pick me up. Your hands are too uncomfortable to hold a steering wheel."

He nodded. "Thanks again for all your help."

❧

Later, after she'd gone, Wendell sat in his office mulling over their conversation. He couldn't help but be impressed by Ophelia's revelation about her brothers. He wanted to ask how they had afforded the expensive education. He knew what he paid his manager, and there was no way he could support a family of nine and send three children to college.

The Trueloves struck him as a resourceful family. Hadn't Ophelia mentioned living with her aunt while attending culinary school? No doubt there were scholarships and student loans as well.

Idly, Wendell massaged his tingling hands with more of the cream she applied earlier. He smiled as he considered her disparaging comment over his tough guy reply. He'd seen her concern, and his heartbeat quickened. He'd wanted to kiss her when he suggested she go home instead.

She'd spoken of her passion for her profession. He understood that passion, the same one he felt for his horses and farm. He needed to steer clear of young Ophelia Truelove. She was getting too close for comfort.

six

What a day. Opie shifted a bag of food to the cart and reached for the next one. Their plan to restock the church's food pantry and aid the food bank had been a huge success. Every family bought more than the five cans per person required for admission to the concert. Opie could hear the roar of the crowd in the background. They sounded as though they enjoyed themselves. Maybe they should make this a regular event.

The planning committee spent a lot of time thinking of ways to increase their pantry supply. One member mentioned the sports events where admission was a toy or cans of food, and they came up with the concert. Another had a friend who sang in a well-known group that was willing to perform. They donated their time in exchange for selling merchandise and gave another 10 percent of their proceeds to the food bank. The committee promoted their generosity and asked those in attendance to support the group that gave so much.

July had been a busy month. Opie placed an advertisement in the paper that resulted in a few personal chef jobs and catered a couple of small events from the kitchen at the big house.

Now that weddings were booked for August, work in the gardens continued at a hectic pace. Val hadn't refused anyone's help, and many days were spent working together to accomplish the goal.

As problems arose with the plans for Val's project, her sister expressed concern over Russ's involvement. Opie thought Val cared more for Russ than she wanted to say. She shared a similar attraction for Wendell, but he obviously didn't feel the same. Lately, she'd seen him when he came to the farm to see her dad and at parties she'd done for people he referred.

"Miss, can I speak with you?"

Opie turned to find a young woman in the doorway. She held a small baby, and two smaller children held on to her legs.

"I saw the sign and I. . ."

She suspected from the woman's demeanor that she needed help and didn't know how to ask. "Please tell me you came to eat some of the sandwiches." Opie prepared a number of cold cut subs to feed the volunteers. More than enough remained to feed this family. "You will help me out, won't you? I hate to see good food go to waste."

A grateful smile touched the woman's face. "My children would love a sandwich."

She took the family over to a table and provided them with plates and napkins. She set the platter in the center. "I wish you'd come earlier when there were more choices."

"These are fine."

Opie stooped down to child level and said, "I have cookies, too, but only if you eat your sandwiches. Would you like chocolate milk?"

Their eyes brightened in the way of kids unused to treats, and her heart hurt for the beautiful children. She pushed the tray toward their mother. "Help yourselves. I'll get the milk." In the church kitchen, she took two cartons each for the children and their mother and returned to find them eating a half sandwich.

"Oh, you have to eat more than that," Opie said as she passed the cartons around. "I'll never get rid of the sandwiches if you don't."

The children looked to their mother with big hopeful eyes, and she placed another sandwich on their plates.

Opie busied herself opening the milk cartons and giving the children straws. "My name is Opie Truelove."

The woman swallowed hurriedly and wiped her hands on her napkin before accepting Opie's hand. "I'm Brenda Clarke. This is Ronnie and Bonnie, and the baby is Shelley."

The boy and girl looked to be the same age. "Are you

twins?" When they nodded, Opie said, "My brothers are twins, too. They're identical."

"We can't be," the boy said. " 'Cause she's a girl."

"No, 'cause you're a boy," his sister countered.

Their mother called their names and they settled down.

She pulled out one of the small chairs and sat down. "It's a pleasure meeting you all. Where do you attend church?"

"My husband works on Sunday. He drives our truck."

"Do you live nearby? We have a church bus if you'd like to attend."

"We live at Hunter Farm. My husband works there."

"Oh, we're neighbors. I live at Sheridan Farm. I know Wendell Hunter."

The woman looked panicked as she stood and stepped away from the table. She beckoned and Opie followed. Her voice dropped low as she said, "Please, miss, don't tell him I came here. Ronald would be so embarrassed. He doesn't mean to take from our children. He just wants to make things better. I tell him it's better if the children eat.

"I can't thank you enough. The children. . ." she began, pausing when she choked up. "They were hungry and I didn't know how I was going to feed them." Tears sprang to her eyes.

Opie pushed a clean paper napkin into her hand. "Don't worry, Brenda. We all have times when we need help. The most important thing is making sure these precious little ones are fed. Do you have formula for the baby?"

"No. I feed her."

"So we need to feed you," Opie said. A nursing mother needed nutrients as well. "There are programs that provide milk and other items for families that qualify. Would you like the information?"

A sad expression covered the young mother's face as she nodded. "Yes, please."

Opie smiled encouragement. "Take your time and eat all you want. Then the children can play while we shop in the pantry. We just stocked it today, and there's plenty of good food for your family. How did you get here?"

"My friend dropped me off. She's going to come back after she runs her errands."

"We'll be ready when she arrives."

Seeing that the children had cleaned their plates, Opie walked over to the counter and picked up the container of chocolate chip cookies she'd baked last night. They eagerly accepted the cookie she handed them, and Opie placed a couple more on their plates.

Later they departed with the remaining sandwiches, groceries, and even cash from Opie's own pocket to use for meats. She'd also given Brenda the number for assistance and urged her to return if she found herself in need again.

Opie repeated her invitation to church and gave the young mother the church's number in case they wanted to ride the bus. She didn't know if she'd ever see the family again, but it pleased Opie to know they would sleep well that night with full stomachs.

A bit of anger toward Wendell welled up in her. How could he live in that big house, eat meals prepared by a chef, and not be aware people were hungry on his farm? Based on what the woman said, Opie suspected the husband might have a problem. Didn't Wendell have any type of personal relationship with the workers on his farm?

God must have sent this young mother her way today. Maybe it was her personal connection with food, but the idea of anyone going hungry bothered Opie a great deal. That's why she volunteered for the food drive and cooked at the shelters.

She said a prayer for the family and completed her tasks, eager to get home. The desire to do more for the family was strong, but Opie knew they needed their pride. She'd provided them with a start tonight.

Her parents told her she couldn't outdo God. Opie knew that, but it would have been hard for her to sit at the table and stuff her face with thoughts of them in need. How many other families suffered in the same way? For a country with so much, there were a number of people with so little.

⤫

As he dressed for the party, Wendell found himself uncertain. When Ophelia invited him to her father's birthday party, he considered whether he should be a good neighbor or refuse. He liked Jacob. In fact, he'd yet to meet a member of this family he didn't like, but his doubts over becoming further involved with them gave him pause.

When the release of information regarding Val's venue business became public, Wendell adopted a wait-and-see attitude. He'd seen a vast improvement in the gardens when he'd visited, and it occurred to him that it might not be what he originally thought. Maybe he should go and see if he could learn more.

The wedding this past weekend hadn't seemed to make a vast difference in traffic. Wendell supposed that would depend on the size of the wedding. He liked his privacy. When someone suggested he should offer farm tours like others in the community, he rejected the idea for that same reason.

When they talked, Ophelia told him she planned to prepare an English tea for Val's launch party and her father's favorites for his birthday on the same day. He'd cautioned her about taking on too much.

Wendell wondered if Russ would be present. If so, tonight could provide an opportunity to interact with his brother.

He asked about her father's likes, and she told him a gift wasn't expected. Wendell disagreed. He'd considered some of the things he liked and settled on a gift card from the local farm supply store.

Ophelia welcomed Wendell and took him over to speak to her dad. When called to the kitchen, she left him with her dad. Jacob sat with his leg propped up and an ice bag resting gingerly against his scalp.

Shocked to find the man battered and bruised, he asked, "What happened?"

"I wish I knew," Jacob said. "Fancy went crazy and kicked me up against the fence."

"Have you been checked out?"

"Don't get them started again," Jacob said quietly. "My head hurts from where I got knocked unconscious and my leg is sore, but I'll survive."

The news troubled Wendell. "And you have no idea what happened?"

"I told them to call in the vet to check Fancy out. I'll let you know what I find out."

"I appreciate that," he said, noting the number of people waiting to speak to Jacob. "We should let your guests offer their birthday wishes."

"I'm glad you came, Wendell."

Russ was present and his evasion skills had improved. Other than the initial cool nod when they first saw each other, his brother gave no indication that Wendell existed. He caught glimpses of him about the room and if Russ was there when Wendell showed up, he quickly moved on. He could only assume Russ's anger increased with the passage of time. Wendell felt no need to be the bigger man.

While Ophelia rushed around finishing her preparations for the meal, Val came over to speak to him. She introduced him to Rom and Heath, and they talked for a while before Heath went off with an attractive young woman named Jane Holt.

"Val tells me you're concerned about how her business will affect the neighborhood," Rom said.

"Traffic is a major concern," Wendell admitted.

Dinner was announced, and Rom accompanied him to the buffet tables. He gestured for him to go first. Wendell picked up a plate and studied the array of foods on the tables. All too soon he'd placed far more than he needed on the plate.

"We can sit over here," Rom said, leading the way. "You don't need to worry. Val plans to bring traffic in off the main road which enables her to give the guests a scenic view and doesn't affect our road at all."

Wendell hadn't considered the possibility of doing that. "Sounds as if it could work."

"It will. You should discuss your concerns with Val. She wants to do what's best for everyone involved."

He'd seen enough effort on Val Truelove's part to believe this to be the case. "I like knowing what's going on in my community."

Rom nodded. "I can understand that."

As he ate, it occurred to Wendell just how different the party atmosphere was from his usual experience. Casual, comfortable, with lots of laughter best described what he witnessed in this room. Most of the guests wore comfortable clothes without designer labels. Respect for all availed. Inexpensive gifts were as appreciated as the more expensive ones. Wendell found it ironic that he and Russ gave the same thing.

"You two must have known I have my eye on a few things down at Joe's," Jacob said, waving the gift cards in the air.

"As every horseman should," he replied.

When the twins showed their father their gift, Wendell admired the horse blankets. The royal blue and gold color combination was impressive with the Truelove Inc. logo. "Nice," he commented to Ophelia when she came to stand by his side.

"They are, aren't they? Val designed that logo."

"I didn't realize she was an artist."

"She calls herself a doodler. She created the design for her business, and we agreed it made a perfect logo for the farm."

"How's your dad doing?"

Wendell broached the subject that controlled his thoughts ever since he learned about the incident. Secretly he had hopes for the foal and Jacob's gut instinct that Fancy could produce a winner. When he learned Jacob owned the filly, his first instinct was to make him an offer. He knew his dad's belief that every horse was for sale would not prove true with this family. Fancy held a special place in her owner's heart. He wanted answers. What caused the incident? Was the horse unstable? Had she ever done this before?

He admired Jacob's horse sense. Back in July, he'd asked Jacob's opinion on a colt he'd found. Where Wendell saw potential with training and time, Jacob wasn't as certain of the animal's abilities. He'd pointed out a couple of things right away that Wendell hadn't seen for himself, and he could only question why. His dad would have noticed those things. Jacob noticed them. Why didn't he? Would he ever develop his horse sense?

"Daddy's tough," she responded. "I'm sure he'll be okay. Did you get enough to eat?"

Wendell laughed. "Are you kidding? You prepared enough to feed a small country."

"There's never enough for that."

Her sad expression made him ask, "What's on your mind?"

"I met someone at the church recently who was having problems feeding her kids. I can't give you a name, but they were associated with your farm. It bothered me that you didn't see their needs."

"Why should I?" Wendell asked, going on to defend himself. "I pay my staff well. Other than rules for those who live on the property, I don't get involved in their personal lives."

"You have to care about what happens to others, Wendell."

Her insistence irritated him. "Why do you think I don't? I provide the job that feeds this person's family. Why is what he does with his money my concern?"

"Because it's the right thing to do," she said, her voice rising. "We have to love our brother."

Wendell looked around to see if anyone had overheard. As far as he was concerned, the only brother he knew didn't want his love. "They're adults, Ophelia. It's their responsibility to manage their funds. If they need a raise, they can discuss it with the manager. I provide them with living accommodations. That's more than most workers get from their employers."

"I think this man might have other issues."

"What sort of issues?" Wendell demanded.

"I don't know, but she said something about him wanting to make things better for his family."

"He could be saving for the future."

"To the extent that his wife and children are hungry?" she asked with disbelief. "That's ridiculous."

"Perhaps she's not good with finances," he suggested.

"I saw them, Wendell. This woman isn't spending money on herself. They were hungry but not greedy when I offered them food. She was desperate enough to take the number of an agency to help her provide for her children."

Seeing she wasn't going to let up, he asked, "What do you want me to do, Ophelia?"

"I want you to care that someone you know might be in trouble."

She wanted too much. If Hunter Farm went under tomorrow, where would those people be? Certainly not worrying about whether he would survive.

"You and your brother avoided each other all evening," she threw out. "If you're like that with him, why would I expect you to be any different with someone else?"

"In case you didn't notice, Russ avoided me." Wendell glanced about and demanded, "Where is he? Maybe you can get your brothers to hold him down while I ask what his problem is."

She touched his arm, her expression one of appeal. "Please don't do anything in anger, Wendell."

He shook her hand off. "I should go. Please extend my wishes to your father."

"Wendell, please don't leave angry."

He refused to look into her pleading gaze, to hear the voice that made him want to do things he never did. "Good night, Ophelia. Thanks for inviting me."

Regardless of what she thought, her news did bother him, and Wendell was determined to find out what was going on with his employee. As for Russ, Wendell couldn't think of a single way to remedy that situation.

20

After their guests left, the family busied themselves with the cleanup. The twins helped their dad to bed and went out to check that the farm had been secured for the night. Jules and the younger boys picked up the living and dining rooms while Opie and Val helped their mom with the dishes. They could see Mom was distracted and sent her to be with their dad.

"Too bad we don't have a dishwasher," Opie said as she slid another stack of plates into the sink.

"We'll have one when we move. Did you plan to paint your room?"

Opie found the idea of moving into the Sheridans' house exciting, particularly the idea of having her own space without leaving home. "No. I like the wallpaper."

Val dried the dish and added it to the stack. "We can start moving our things anytime. After the wedding this weekend, we'll work on the rest of the house." She polished a plate with the drying cloth for a minute or two before she spoke. "I need to talk to you about Wendell."

Had Val heard them arguing earlier? Opie regretted what she'd said. Her timing stunk. "What about him?"

"I told Russ we can never be more than friends tonight. He didn't take it well."

She shared a sympathetic smile and wondered where Wendell fitted into the discussion.

"He was angry when he said it, but Russ said I should warn you about Wendell. He said Wendell has less use for religion than he does."

Opie concentrated on rinsing the plate and stood it in the drain. "Wendell has issues, but I know God can change him."

"Yes, God can. You can't," Val warned.

"I care for him," Opie said.

"You're attracted to him. I knew you were interested the first time you showed me his photo."

She sighed. "I didn't think I'd feel this way."

"We have to be strong. Trying to take matters into our own hands will only make us more miserable in the end."

Opie refused to stop trying. Wendell needed someone who cared in a major way. "I'm not giving up. If anyone needs to hear God's message, it's Wendell. If I walk away, he won't."

"You don't know that. Please don't look at him as a challenge, Opie."

"I'm not," she protested. She planned to follow God's leading in the matter.

"You show no fear in confronting Wendell. Did it occur to you that you could be making matters worse?"

"Like saying 'we can only be friends' to a man who indicates his interest in you is going to improve your situation?"

"I was honest with Russ."

Opie wiped down the countertops. "How is this going to impact your project?"

"I can only hope he's professional enough to separate his personal life from his business. Just be careful, Opie."

"I know what I'm doing, Val."

seven

Those words were still on her mind the following morning. She owed Wendell an apology. After breakfast, she took the cordless and slipped outside to make the call. "Hi. It's Opie. I'm sorry about last night," she said when he answered. "I shouldn't have said anything."

She expected him to tear into her. In fact, she couldn't blame him if he did. She knew better than to antagonize a guest in their home.

"It's different for us, Ophelia," Wendell said with quiet emphasis. "We weren't raised in the same nurturing environment you have."

"What happened?" She sat in the swing and nudged it into motion. When he didn't say anything, Opie thought she'd overstepped her boundaries again.

"Russ didn't take well to learning he didn't inherit a portion of the farm. Our father died without making us aware of the true situation."

That caught her attention. She leaned forward, bringing the movement to a sudden halt. "What situation?"

"My dad and I didn't have the best relationship. He didn't know what to do with me. Then Nicole came along, and she was more interested in having fun than in mothering a child who wasn't hers. Dad hired a succession of nannies and left me behind while they traveled to races and took vacations. Between nannies, Dad sent me to stay with my mom's parents."

"Did they like your father?" Opie wished she had gone to his house for this conversation.

"No. They never wanted her to marry him. My parents eloped."

It sounded as if his mom had a mind of her own.

"They didn't disown her?"

"No. She was their only child. My grandparents gave Stryker-Steele Farm to my mother as a wedding gift. She changed the name, but they stipulated the farm would go to her firstborn son in the event of her death."

Opie didn't understand. "Why would they do that?"

"She struggled with breathing issues as a child. I suppose the doctors might have given them some warning."

"Does Russ know about their stipulation?"

"No. He never gave me an opportunity to explain. Dad met Nicole at the tracks. He brought her here, and they lived together until my grandparents threatened to take me away. Nicole became pregnant around the same time, and they married. Russ's birth impeded her travels. Dad wasn't about to drag a newborn along. When he left for the races, she concentrated on removing every trace of my mother from the house. She even tried to get him to sell the place, but he refused. She took her frustrations out on me."

His situation tore at her heart. How lonely he must have been. Not only had he lost his mother but his father, as well. "Why did she dislike you so?"

"It was what I represented," he said. Opie noted the faint tremor in his voice. "My father loved my mother, and Nicole felt threatened. Maybe she would have been nicer if she'd known the farm was mine. Then again, there's no telling what she would have done if she had."

Opie gasped at his sarcastic laugh. "Didn't anyone see how she treated you?"

"Nicole was careful. She staged incidents so that I came off as the brat. After a while, I decided to play her game. I was crying out for attention, but my dad was too blind to see.

"They sent me off to boarding school. I was a behavioral problem until one of the counselors listened and became like a big brother to me. After that, I didn't want to come back. Dad would show up and make me come home. I think my grandparents must have insisted he be a better father, and he was afraid they would put him off the farm if he didn't."

"Did you tell them what was going on?"

"No. They were getting older and not in the best of health, and I knew they weren't up to a fight against my dad. After he died, I understood why he kept me around."

"I'm sure he loved you, Wendell."

His snort indicated he lacked her certainty. "After I finished college, he proposed we get to know each other. In my ignorance, I thought he wanted to spend time together. Now I believe they told him he needed to train me. He did, but he didn't plan to give up the reins any time soon."

"How could he keep it a secret? Why didn't your grandparents do something?"

"What choice did they have? I was his trump card. If they sent him away, they lost their only grandchild. Then after my grandfather died, my grandmother went to live with her sister in France."

"I'm sorry, Wendell."

"Makes you appreciate your parents, doesn't it?"

"Oh, I'm very thankful for them both. We've always been wealthy in the things that truly mattered."

"I'd choose loving parents any day," Wendell agreed.

"You say Russ won't let you explain?"

"Russ took his things and left a note one weekend when I was away. That's the last I've seen or heard of him until the party last night. He doesn't want to hear the truth. It's his choice."

"Does that mean you don't care?"

"He's my brother, Ophelia. We're not close, but I prefer he not hate me for something outside my control. I'd like for him to understand, but if he's determined not to listen, it's not likely I'll ever tell him the truth."

"He'll listen one day, Wendell."

"Maybe. What are you doing today?"

"As little as possible." Tired from the previous day's events, she planned to relax.

"Would you like to visit the Horse Park?"

Opie could only wonder why he invited her. Her first thought would be that he'd keep his distance after her last attack. "Are you playing tourist?"

"I have to conduct a bit of business, but I wouldn't mind touring the site."

"I haven't been there in years. What time?"

"I'm meeting with my manager in a few minutes. Let's say ten thirty?"

"I'll be ready."

❧

Wendell hung up. Why had he shared all that with Opie? Maybe because he wanted her to understand he wasn't a bad person.

"Hey boss, you wanted to see me?"

Wendell gestured his farm manager in. He sat down at his desk and reached for a pen. "How many young families do we have on the farm?"

"Maybe three or four."

"Any of them exhibiting financial problems?"

"Not that I've heard, but then it's not likely they would share that kind of information."

"Anyone asked for a raise lately?"

Jack Pitt shrugged. "Hints but no outright requests."

"I want to know if you hear anything. And I want this kept between us." Wendell resolved to do his own detective work. He didn't care for looking bad in situations outside his control. He paid his men, and what they did with the money was their concern so long as they weren't into anything that could affect his farm. "What about gambling? Anyone you think might have a problem?"

"Most place bets at the tracks."

"Does anyone regularly borrow money to get them through to their next check?"

The man's brow furrowed. "Now that you mention it, someone mentioned young Clarke borrowing money before his last check. You think he's in financial trouble?"

"I don't know. We need to keep our eyes and ears open." Wendell knew that employees with financial problems were more likely to cave in to temptations.

"Clarke has a wife and three small kids," Jack said. "I attributed it to him having the family, but it could be something else. He's young. Midtwenties. Hard worker. Eager to get ahead in life."

"Does he bet?"

Another shrug. "I could ask around."

Wendell didn't need convincing. He knew this was his man. "No. Keep it between us. Report back if anything comes to your attention. If he has a problem, I'll see to it that he gets help before it gets out of control. His family should come first."

"I agree. Taking a wife and having children is a responsibility only a man should assume."

He agreed with the manager. "Does he drink? Go out at night?"

"He strikes me as a family man. If anything, he's probably trying to win the big one and get ahead in life."

"Difficult to do when one income supports five people."

You'd think we'd learn, Wendell thought, realizing the same applied to him. He kept trying for the big one, hoping to prove himself worthy of being his father's son. He'd been more fortunate financially than the young man, but at least young Clarke had a wife and family. More than he could say for himself.

When had he put his hunt for Mrs. Right on hold? He hadn't given up totally, but there were things that needed doing first. Was he really too busy, or did it have more to do with wanting something or someone he couldn't have?

Spending time with a loving family with hearts big enough to encompass each other and their friends was nice. He regretted arguing with Ophelia. She couldn't help caring about people. It was her nature.

❧

The hot August day made Opie wonder if she'd made the wisest choice. After their earlier conversation, the idea of spending more time with Wendell appealed to her. She needed him to see she cared for him as a friend. She truly regretted arguing with him. Val had a point. She had to stop confronting him over her beliefs or she'd push him away forever.

Located half an hour outside Paris, the Kentucky Horse Park promoted itself as the only park dedicated to man's relationship with the horse. She'd taken a few minutes to tour their Web site while she waited for Wendell.

They parked and strolled toward the building, their eyes going immediately to the huge painting of horses running the water with the slogan, THOU SHALT FLY WITHOUT WINGS, above the doors. They went inside and made plans to meet later.

Wendell left to conduct his business, and Opie went back outside to enjoy the area. She snapped photos of the impressive statues with her digital camera. After awhile, she used the admission ticket Wendell bought to visit the International Museum of the Horse. She read histories; viewed tack and hardware, wagons, displays; and concluded with the history of some of the most popular horses ever to race. After finishing, she went back out to the visitor information center and found him waiting.

"How was the museum?"

"Informative."

"I can't think of a better place for the park. There have been horses here for more than two hundred years. What did you plan to do next?" he asked.

She unfolded her visitor map, and they viewed the schedule of activities. "Let's take the Horse Drawn Trolley Ride and go see the Parade of Breeds."

They also visited the Hall of Champions and American Saddlebred Museum and managed to fit the *Thou Shalt Fly Without Wings* film into the schedule. As she listened to Wendell, she realized she'd heard that same excitement when her dad talked horses.

"Had enough?" he asked when they exited the film.

Opie nodded, and they strolled toward the main gate. "I need to remind Heath about this place. Sammy loves horses."

"She could ride the ponies."

"You should see how excited she gets when we take her to the barn." She paused to admire two foal statues. "The statuary is great."

"It is. I've thought about commissioning a piece for the farm but never have."

"You should. It's beautiful work. Maybe a couple of smaller pieces at the entrance."

He nodded. "Before I forget, are you available to prepare a dinner next Tuesday night? I'm having a birthday dinner party for Catherine and Jean-Pierre has the flu."

"He's having a difficult time lately," Opie commented. She wondered about the woman Wendell cared enough for to throw a party.

"He is," Wendell agreed. "It's Catherine's thirtieth birthday. She wasn't going to do anything, but we insisted on marking the occasion."

"We?" she asked.

"Her husband Leo and myself. We attended private school together. They're in real estate. Cat's the one who talked me into the bachelor auction."

Relief surged through Opie. "Any ideas on the menu? A cake?"

"Actually she'd prefer those desserts you prepared last time. She still talks about how good they were. I know it's not much time."

"I'll come over Tuesday morning and get everything together."

They arrived at the car, and Wendell unlocked the door for her. "Thanks, Ophelia. By the way, I think I figured out who came to the church."

Her head jerked about. "You didn't say anything, did you?"

"No, but I plan to keep my eyes and ears open. Employees with financial troubles can be a liability in my business. My source says this particular young man is eager to get ahead, and I hope he's not going about it the wrong way."

She'd never considered that aspect. "Wendell, please don't

embarrass his wife. She's doing the best she can."

He looked at her for several seconds. "That's never been my intention, Ophelia."

Opie smiled. She believed him. "Thanks, Wendell."

eight

After dinner that night, Opie and Val started moving boxes to the truck. Opie would miss the home where she'd grown up. She'd been the first child born after they moved to the manager's house, and she remained there until she went off to culinary school.

After her first trip to her new bedroom, Opie veered off to the kitchen. The Sheridans renovated the old kitchen, turning it into a huge commercial-type kitchen with granite countertops and quality appliances. A few things were a little outdated, but Opie knew it was going to be one of her favorite rooms in the house.

"There you are," Val said when she walked into the room. "I should have known."

"You think there's enough room in this kitchen for two cooks?"

She glanced around. "Should be, but you and Mom will have to come to an agreement."

"I know."

"So you went to the Horse Park with Wendell today," Val said.

Opie nodded. She'd mentioned it over dinner, telling Heath he needed to take Sammy. The mention of horses set the little girl off, and she'd talked nonstop until Heath promised to take her to the barn after dinner.

"I called this morning to apologize, and he really opened up about his past. Said Russ wouldn't listen when he tried to tell him his mother's will stipulated the farm go to her firstborn son. Their dad never told them about the will. I wish I could help them work out their relationship."

"Pray. God could make you their mediator. Come on. We

need to unload those boxes. I have a busy day tomorrow."

"Need help with the wedding?"

"An extra set of hands is always appreciated."

"Wendell asked me to prepare a dinner party for his friend's birthday Tuesday night, but that shouldn't be too hard."

"Opie, about what Wendell told you. . . You're not. . ."

"I told you, Val. I just want to be his friend."

Even as she spoke the words, Opie knew she wanted to be far more to Wendell.

Heath and Jane took Monday off and went into Paris. Opie and Val worked on sorting their belongings and deciding what to take with them. With two successful weddings and the launch party under her belt, Val was thrilled with her progress.

Tuesday morning, Opie prepared for Wendell's event while the others started to move the family. She was leaving when her father called to say Heath and Sammy fell down the stairs. She hurried over to find them both badly injured and in a great deal of pain. Heath told the emergency personnel to take Sammy and Jane in the ambulance. He would ride in the SUV with their security. The attendants immobilized his leg and helped get him inside. He was white by the time they finished.

"I have to be over at Wendell's all day," Opie told Val before they left. "His party is tonight."

"Take your phone. I'll keep you updated. I'll leave a message if you don't answer."

Opie trailed her to the vehicle, torn between family and commitment. "I'd cancel, but Jean-Pierre is sick."

"Do the job, Opie. He won't be alone. We have to go."

She leaned inside the vehicle and touched his arm. "I love you, Heath. I'm praying."

He nodded and closed his eyes.

Wendell was coming out of the house when she arrived. "Sorry I'm late. Heath tripped over Sammy on the stairs this morning."

"Are they okay?" Wendell asked.

"They think she broke her arm. Heath broke his leg. He

was moving a big box and didn't see her."

"Do you need to go? I can take my guests out to dinner."

Opie shook her head. "The family is with him, and Val said she'd keep me informed. I'd rather be busy here than worried at the hospital."

"Let me know if anything changes," he said. "Do you need anything?"

"Is April around today? I could use an extra set of hands."

"Ask Mrs. Carroll to call her."

"I will." She smiled her thanks to Glenn, the security staff member who brought her bag of produce from the vehicle.

"The farmers market must love you," Wendell commented doing a quick save when a couple of zucchini fell from the bag. He tucked them back inside.

"Actually this came from a friend's garden. She shared with Mom, and she told me to take the excess."

"Thank them both for me."

"Just wait until you taste the great things I do with them."

"I look forward to it," he said.

"You'll be planting your own garden next year."

Opie stayed busy. Val called a couple of times to say they were waiting on X-rays and doctors and promised to let her know as soon as they knew something definite. Since she hadn't heard from her again, she could only assume they were still waiting.

Though curious about Wendell's friends, Opie blocked out the party and concentrated on getting the food out. After serving the dessert course, she took a moment to call and check on Heath.

"He's spending the night at the hospital," Val said. "They casted Sammy's arm and sent her home with Jane. She's not a happy baby, but she's okay."

"Thank God for that."

"Are you almost finished?"

"I just sent out the last of it," Opie said. "I need to clean up before heading for the hospital."

"You might as well go home. Heath is pretty much out of it. I think we're all going to head that way shortly."

"Okay, I'll see you soon." Wendell and a woman stepped into the room. "Gotta go. Wendell's just come in."

"That was Val," she explained as she slipped the phone into her pocket.

"How are Heath and Sammy?"

"He's staying at the hospital tonight. They casted Sammy's arm and sent her home."

He grimaced. "Sorry. Ophelia, this is Susan Boone. She wanted to meet you."

Susan Boone smiled up at him, never releasing her hold on Wendell's arm. Opie recognized her from the social pages. Her family came from old Kentucky money and supported a number of charities and foundations. She was closer to the twins' age and from the looks of her, a perfect match for Wendell's wish list.

"I just loved your food," she enthused. "I'd like to engage your services to cater an event next month. We're between chefs, and I think this could be the perfect solution."

Opie pulled a business card from her pocket. "Give me a call, and we'll discuss the particulars."

Wendell smiled at Susan and patted her hand. "Go back to the party. I'll be there after I speak with Ophelia."

"Nice meeting you. Hurry back," she told Wendell, pausing to kiss his cheek.

Opie watched her leave the room and asked, "Miss Right?"

"I've known Susan and her family for years. You should go ahead and leave. I can get Mrs. Carroll to handle this."

"I'll finish up here and head home."

Wendell glanced toward the door. "I have to get back to my guests. Take off whenever you need to. Thanks for doing this at the last minute."

"It's my job."

"Don't you mean career?"

"Yes, my career."

After he'd gone, Opie concentrated on finishing service. All too soon, the tears trailed down her cheeks. Why had she allowed this to happen? Wendell hadn't lied to her about what he wanted in life. She knew she didn't stand a chance. Why did it hurt so much?

Opie called security, finished packing up her knives, and walked out to the waiting SUV. After catching up on Heath, she went to prepare for bed.

"What's wrong?" Val asked when she came out of the bathroom. "Why are you moping around?"

"I'm not."

Val's doubt-filled expression disputed her response. Her sister's ability to read her so well was definitely a negative of close families.

"It's Wendell."

"What about him? I thought you were pleased that he gave you another job."

"I was. I thought maybe he'd reconsidered about working women."

"What happened?" Val asked.

"He had a date. Susan Boone."

"What are you going to do, Opie?"

"Nothing. He's out of my league. He has money. Social standing."

"You have money."

"Not like those women he dates. They're blue-blooded down to their expensive pointy-toed heels. He brought her into the kitchen to meet me. She raved about the food and said he'd told her I was a personal chef. They're between chefs, and she wants to book an event next month."

"That's good news, isn't it?"

"I suppose," Opie said, wishing she could tell the woman no.

"Take care, little sister," Val warned. "Wendell Hunter

appeals to you, and you're blinding yourself to reality."

"I know it can't be, Val. That doesn't mean I can't appreciate his finer qualities."

"That second and third look is often what gets you in over your head. You start thinking you can change the things you can't. Please don't make me wish I'd never bought you that date."

Opie didn't tell Val she wished she'd never read the magazine article that started all this. Life was so much simpler before Wendell Hunter came into her life.

nine

"Where did you say your mother is?" Jacob Truelove requested when Opie set the plate of food on the table before him.

"At church. Her woman's group is having a luncheon. I promised I'd feed you."

When she planned chow mein for lunch, Opie hadn't realized her father would invite Wendell to join them. At least he'd given her a bit of warning when he called up to the house to tell her to set another place at the table.

After grace, Jacob took a bite and asked, "What did you say this is?"

Opie glanced at Wendell, wondering what he thought. In today's world, most people ate Chinese cuisine on a regular basis. "It's chicken chow mein. Do you want me to fix you something else?"

"No," Jacob said with a shake of his head. "This is tasty. What's this?" he asked, lifting a sprout with his fork. "Looks like grass."

She felt her skin growing warm. "It's a bean sprout. They're good for you."

"Did you think Opie was feeding you horse food, Dad?"

Opie would have thumped Heath if he hadn't already been in pain. He had come home from the hospital the day before. Because of his limited mobility, she offered to take his food into the family room, but he insisted on coming to the table. He sat with his casted leg propped up on an extra chair.

"Heath," Jane admonished as she paused in feeding Sammy. "Opie worked hard to make this food for us."

"Not really," she admitted. "But Heath obviously prefers horse food to hospital food."

Val laughed and high-fived her. Heath grinned.

"You kids behave," Jacob ordered. "Wendell will think we didn't teach you any manners." He glanced at their guest. "They pick on Opie's cooking all the time, but I've never seen anyone leave the table yet."

Wendell smiled. "You're lucky to have her. She's been a big hit with my guests."

"This family has been blessed with good cooks." Jacob glanced at Opie and said, "If your mom's schedule gets any fuller, I might have to hire you to cook for us."

"You can't afford me."

He pretended shock. "You'd charge your old dad?"

Everyone chuckled when she promised to give him a good rate.

"Believe me, she's worth every penny she charges," Wendell said.

His statement rated up there with the highest praise she'd ever received. Opie shut everyone out as she focused on Wendell. "So you understand why I have to cook?"

He met and held her gaze. "I respect that you do what you love."

"That should be the same for every woman," she said.

Heath groaned. "Don't get her started on equality for women."

Opie shot him a warning look. "You're awfully brave for a man with a cast on his leg."

"We've had this discussion before, and we're not going to have it again now, are we, Ophelia? Your father invited me to share your lunch, but I won't disrupt the meal with a disagreement."

"I'm not trying to start an argument," she protested. "I just want everyone to understand my work is important to me."

"We know that, Opie," Val said. "In fact, we feel blessed to enjoy the results of your work."

"You're doing what God intended for you," her dad added. "And you'll use that talent in the way He intends whether you're a homemaker like your mother or the next famous chef."

She played with the food on her plate as the others changed

the topic. Her growing feelings for Wendell made her consider the prospect of becoming a homemaker. Could she be happy preparing meals for him and their family and guests? For that matter, would he allow her to do that? Or insist on a chef?

"Opie, did you hear Daddy?"

Val's question made her look up. "I'm sorry. What?"

"He asked if there's any dessert left from last night."

She pushed her chair back and stood. "I made a cake. I'll get it."

"I'll help," Val said.

Opie picked up their plates and carried them into the kitchen.

"Are you okay?" Val asked.

"Yeah, I'm fine." She stacked dessert plates, cups, and saucers on a tray. One of the cups toppled and shattered on the tile floor. She started to sob as she knelt on the floor.

Val knelt by her side, one hand resting on her shoulder. "Opie?"

"No, I'm not okay," she declared. "I've done something really stupid."

"What? Stop before you cut yourself," Val ordered when Opie fumbled the pieces. "I'll get the broom."

She left them on the floor and stood. "I let myself fall in love with a man who doesn't want me."

"Oh, Opie." Val pulled her into a hug.

"Everything okay in there?" her dad called out.

"Yes," Val responded. "We dropped a cup." She turned and reached for the cake stand. "Take your time. I'll serve this."

Opie wiped her eyes and said, "I can do it." She balanced the tray on one arm, grabbed the coffee carafe from the counter, and led the way. Val followed with the cake.

"It's pecan fudge delight." Wendell's favorite. She hadn't realized he'd be there when she made the dessert that morning.

He grinned. "It must be my lucky day."

"You keep cooking like this and some man is going to steal you away." Her father winked at her.

"I plan to get better," Opie assured as she sliced the cake with deft, precise cuts. "Cooking is my life."

She served them, leaving Heath until last. "I shouldn't give you any after that grass comment."

"Please. 'Cause you love me."

His pitiful plea made her laugh, and she cut an extra large piece. She hugged him as she set the plate down on the table. "I do love you, and I'm glad you're home."

After the others left the table, Opie collected the dishes and carried them into the kitchen.

Wendell returned to place a check on the counter. "I didn't get a chance to give you that before you left the other night."

"I wanted to check on Heath."

"I know. Everyone raved about your food. Don't be surprised if some of those business cards you displayed so discreetly result in more work."

She'd placed a basket of hand-dipped chocolates on the table by his front door with a holder of business cards. "Too obvious?" she asked.

"I'd say nice touch. The candy was delicious by the way. I forgot your basket and holder."

She laughed. "Thanks. I'll pick it up soon."

Wendell propped against the island. "Susan said you weren't able to cater her event."

She called Opie the morning after the party. After hearing Susan Boone's plans, she told her it wasn't possible. "I don't have a kitchen large enough to prepare for a group that size."

"What do you need?"

"A commercial kitchen. She's planning on between two and three hundred people. And I'd have to hire staff."

"You don't want the event?"

"I won't take on a job I can't complete."

"Susan was disappointed."

She shrugged. "In a few months, I'll have the kitchen at the pavilion and will be able to take on bigger jobs. Maybe she'll give me another chance."

Wendell accepted her excuse. "Ophelia, what was your objective with that confrontation at lunch?"

She fiddled with the cloth she picked up from the countertop. "I let myself hope."

"Hope?" he repeated.

Her need to make him understand shocked her. "That maybe you'd wake up and see that what you think you want isn't how it has to be."

"You mean us? It wouldn't work Ophelia." His head moved in a slow back-and-forth sideways.

"I'm all wrong for you. I'm too old."

"You're not that old," she protested. Opie meant what she'd told Val about age. She didn't care that Wendell was older than her.

"We're too different in all the ways that count."

"How can you know that? Do you really know me?" she asked, staring at him.

"I know your values. I know what you want out of life. It wouldn't work."

"You think you know me so well, but you don't," she argued, turning away from him.

"I know you better than you realize. I know you'd never do anything to hurt your family, which would happen if you became involved with an old sinner like me."

Opie tossed the dishcloth into the sink and whirled back to face him. "You don't have to be that way, Wendell. God loves you. Accepting Him as your Savior would make you happier than you've ever been."

"I don't feel unhappy."

Frustrated, she cried, "Because you're blind to your misery. You hate a loving God for what happened to your mom. Did it ever occur to you that He didn't want her to die? That He gave her freedom of choice and she chose not to go to the doctor?

"You said yourself that you never had a good relationship with your father, and you're heading down that same path with Russ. If you don't stop and take a long look at yourself, you'll probably marry a woman who can't make you happy and produce children who won't love and respect their father either."

He pushed himself upright, standing stiffly. "You don't know that."

"I know that people who are always searching for personal happiness don't care who they hurt in the process."

"Don't judge me, Ophelia."

She couldn't begin to imagine his life, but Opie wanted so much for him. "I care for you, Wendell. I want to see you happier than you've ever been. Life has its ups and downs, but when you claim God as your Father, you have someone to turn to in the tough times."

Heath swung into the kitchen on his crutches. "Opie, can you help me. . ." He paused. "Sorry. I didn't realize you were still here."

"That's okay. I was on my way out." He glanced at her and said, "Thanks for lunch. It was delicious as usual."

Heath noted Wendell's hasty departure before turning to her. "What was that about?"

She wasn't ready to discuss this. "He wanted to give me a check. What did you need?"

After she helped Heath locate the acetaminophen, Opie returned to the kitchen and started preparations for dinner. She was fixing the roast when her mom returned and asked how things had gone.

"Daddy seemed to like the stir fry. He invited Wendell Hunter to join us."

"Oh," her mother voiced her surprise. "I didn't realize he planned to invite anyone to lunch."

"He didn't. Wendell stopped by and Daddy asked him to stay."

"I'm sure everything was fine. Thank you, Opie."

"You're welcome, Mom. How was your luncheon?"

They discussed the event, and Opie could see her mother enjoyed her outing. "You should do things more often. I don't mind helping out."

"You're a big help, and I probably don't tell you thanks often enough."

"You don't need to thank me. I love doing things for you. Always have."

Her mother touched her cheek with the gentleness that only a mother could share. "Your father and I have been tremendously blessed with our children. I listen to others request prayer for their wayward children, and I feel I should fall to my knees and thank the Lord for all He's given me."

Her words reminded Opie that she needed to turn to God for her answers. Sometimes she forgot to practice what she preached.

ten

September moved on and Opie's life got even busier. She hadn't seen Wendell since the day he came to lunch. Realizing she didn't have the answers, she placed the situation in God's hands and did her best not to force the issue. Even though her belief she could help never wavered, there were times when Opie doubted she could get beyond her feelings for him.

"Any word from Prestige?" Opie asked Val over breakfast. They were all struggling with a recent incident concerning the pavilion project that had thrown Russ into a very bad light. He denied sending the contractor the e-mail changing the concrete pour and Opie believed him.

"Russ called to say Randall King is looking into the situation."

Opie frowned. She knew Val didn't have good feelings about the owner of the architectural firm that employed Russ. "What does that mean?"

"I'm sure he's looking at things from a liability aspect."

"Any more problems?" She spread a thin layer of jelly on her slice of toast and took a bite.

"No. Todd says Russ is watching things like a hawk. I think he's afraid someone's out to hurt me and determined they won't."

Fear rose up in Opie's throat, the toast nearly choking her as she considered Val's words. "Why haven't you told me this before? That's crazy. What have you done to anyone to cause this?"

"I won the lottery."

"Right. You won," she agreed, shoving the plate away. "What you do with the money is your concern. You aren't hurting anyone with your plans."

"But whoever is behind this feels entitled to share in my

wealth. I just hope Russ can prove his innocence. It doesn't look good."

"Why did you give him another chance?"

"Because he asked and gave me a reason to believe I should."

Opie knew Val cared for Russ a lot and hoped they could work things out.

She hadn't given a lot of thought to work until Susan Boone called again.

"Wendell says you refused because you don't have a large enough kitchen?"

"That's right."

"I have an idea. My friend owns a restaurant downtown. He's willing to rent the space to you from midnight until around five a.m. Would that work?"

Her suggestion puzzled Opie. "Why are you going out of your way like this? Surely you know other caterers."

"Wendell says I won't be disappointed, and I believe him."

Opie appreciated his support, but she didn't understand why he had gone back to Susan with what she'd told him. Why was it so important that she cater this event? She weighed the pros and cons and said, "Give me your friend's number. If we can work things out, I'll be happy to cater your event." She scribbled the name and number on a scrap of paper.

"Wendell said you did an English tea party for your sister. Would you be willing to do a themed party for me?"

"Name your theme, and I'll plan the menu."

Opie promised to get back to her as soon as possible. She was able to work a deal with Ken Brown and called to let Susan know.

"I'm so glad," Susan said. "Wendell will be happy that you're catering the engagement party."

Opie's heart plummeted. No wonder Wendell claimed he wasn't right for her. He'd already found his Mrs. Right. A wealthy, perfect woman who befitted his social status. Never a rebellious upstart who didn't know when to shut up.

Her heart took another hit when Susan said she wanted a costume ball. The theme would be romance, and their guests would come dressed as famous lovers throughout the ages.

Opie didn't want to see Wendell in the role of another woman's lover, famous or not. She wanted him for herself. She forced herself to listen as Susan named a few specific menu items she wanted.

"I'm giving you free rein with the rest of the food."

"I'll get the menu and cost projections to you by the end of the week."

"Thanks, Ophelia. I want this to be the party everyone remembers."

"It will be." Opie knew she'd never forget the event.

She threw herself into her work, determined to make Wendell's engagement party unforgettable. Though she wanted to dislike the woman he'd chosen, Opie found Susan to be very likeable and easy to work with. No doubt they would call on her for future work. The idea gnawed at Opie. How could she cater events for the man she loved and another woman? She pushed the idea away. She'd cross that bridge in the future. Maybe this was God's way of directing her path elsewhere.

The strong temptation to confront Wendell ate at Opie. He'd said he'd known Susan for years, but why had she never been present at the events when she'd cooked for him and his guests? What kind of relationship did he have with his future wife? She wanted answers.

Yet, Opie knew she had no rights where Wendell was concerned. He'd made no promises to her. He hadn't led her on. It wasn't fair to him or to her to pursue the matter. Wendell had made his decision. A realist, she allowed herself to cry for what she couldn't have but refused to embarrass him or herself with further declarations of love. Opie held firm and as the week for preparation arrived, she only grew more despondent. While she worked, she fantasized about ways to convince him to change his mind.

Opie planned to take a week to prepare for the event. She

hired sufficient staff, and her lists grew by the day. Her assistants worked the same long night hours. Opie was thankful when Susan's friend offered her the use of an empty walk-in fridge to store the items until the night of the party.

At times, she feared she'd never complete service, but as always everything fell into place. On the night of the party, she took a moment to step out into the Boones' drawing room to see the happy couple. Maybe seeing Wendell in love would help her accept the situation. She really did want his happiness.

The room sparkled with understated elegance, taking Susan's theme of romance far from the Valentine-red heart variety. Candles and ambient lighting, fine china, heirloom silver, crystal stemware, and masses of red roses filled the long buffet tables. Servers stood ready to fill the guests' plates.

This was every woman's dream—the perfect event and the perfect man.

Opie spotted Wendell talking with a couple of people over by the french doors. His lack of costume surprised her. Surely, he wouldn't break Susan's heart by refusing to participate in her party theme. She looked around and spotted Susan dressed as Cinderella. Another man dressed as Prince Charming stood with his arm about her waist. How could Wendell stand by while another man took his place on the most important night of his life? Opie walked to where Wendell now stood alone.

"Why aren't you wearing your Prince Charming costume?"

"I can't see me in that getup. I opted to come as myself."

She sniffed. "You hardly qualify as a world's greatest lover. Why aren't you with Susan?"

"I doubt she'd care for my intrusion on her romantic moment." He took a sip from his glass.

"But it's your engagement party."

Liquid sprayed from his lips as Wendell's brows arched. "What are you talking about? I'm not marrying Susan."

"You let me believe you cared for her." Opie sucked in a deep breath as it occurred to her that she'd made the wrong assumption. Grabbing a napkin, she patted at the wet spots on her coat. She handed him a napkin. "You knew I'd think it was you when she said engagement party."

She heard his quick intake of breath.

"I never indicated any relationship with Susan beyond our friendship. You came to that conclusion on your own."

"But you knew I thought. . ."

"It's not me, Ophelia. What does it matter, anyway?" he asked as if bored with the conversation.

"You know why. She loves you."

"She does. As a friend. We dated a few times before I introduced her to Tony."

She frowned, unsure about what she was hearing. "She dumped you for your friend?"

"No. She didn't dump me." He sounded exasperated by her assumptions. "We never had that kind of relationship."

"So you're okay with her marrying your friend?"

He shrugged. "They make a great couple."

Embarrassed, Opie said, "I need to get back to the kitchen. Enjoy the party."

"You've done an excellent job, Ophelia. I can see your career taking off after tonight."

Opie mumbled thanks and pushed through her confused emotions to complete service.

❧

Her bookings did increase. Susan asked her to do a charity event, and over the next couple of weeks Opie received a number of calls from people who wanted a private chef to prepare a special dinner. Ken agreed to continue their working arrangement for the charity event, but Opie knew she needed her own place if she wanted to carry out her other plan as well. She'd catered the dinner events from her customers' kitchens and then gone on to the restaurant after closing hours to prepare for the bigger party.

"How did it go?" Val asked when they passed each other in the yard.

She'd worked all night and felt comfortable with her

accomplishments. "I'm ready for tonight's party."

"What did you find out about the storefront you looked at?"

"We're negotiating. The owner wants more than I'm willing to invest. I'd have to renovate the kitchen. I wish the pavilion were ready. That would be perfect."

"Renting the restaurant kitchen has worked out okay, hasn't it?"

"Yeah, but hauling supplies in and rushing to clean up before they open for breakfast is difficult. I need a place that opens for lunch."

"How can you work all night and still be together for the event?"

Her back ached between her shoulders, and her eyes burned from exhaustion. "I'll be fine. Lots of kids my age burn the candle at both ends."

"Have you decided if you're going with us next week?"

Now that the plan to visit their grandfather was definite, Opie struggled with doubts about meeting him. She felt no bond or respect, nor had she ever seen any indication her dad cared about a relationship with his father. "Part of me thinks we should let it go. Daddy's lived with it this long."

"That doesn't sound like you," Val protested. "You always want to right the wrongs of the world."

"When I see a wrong," she agreed. "I prayed over your request, but I think we're making more problems for ourselves."

Val appeared disappointed by her decision. "We don't know him well enough to think anything, Opie. I haven't seen him since I was a child, and I certainly don't remember him."

"Tell me again why you feel the need to do this."

"For Daddy. You don't have to go. The twins plan to come."

"I didn't say I wouldn't go," she protested. She was part of this family, and if the visit benefited their dad, she'd support him 100 percent. "I just want to know what you hope to accomplish. You're forcing Daddy to do something he doesn't want to do."

"I didn't force him," Val protested. "I told him I planned

to visit and gave him the option to come if he wanted."

"You knew he wouldn't say no." They both knew their protective father.

"Aren't you curious? He's our grandfather."

"Not really. He's not like Grammy, Uncle Zeb, and Aunt Karen. They're Daddy's family who we know and love."

"And your heart isn't big enough to love a stranger?"

Val's comment hit home. This stranger's blood flowed through their veins. "You know it is."

"I feel God wants me to do something. You didn't see how upset Daddy was."

Opie had witnessed her dad's controlled anger a few times, but she'd never seen him out of control. Evidently learning his father knew about the lottery winnings pushed him over the edge.

"Haven't you ever noticed how Daddy acts after they talk on the phone?" Val asked.

"He doesn't have much to say."

"Because he's so angry with Grandfather he can hardly bear to speak to him. Daddy's asked me not to do things, but he's never forbidden me before. I didn't plan to give Grandfather money, but Daddy spoke to me as if I were a small child. Said he couldn't stop Grammy, but he could stop me. Does that sound like Daddy to you?"

"No," Opie agreed.

"I need to see why Daddy is afraid of him."

"Are you nuts? If a big strong man like our father has fears, you don't think you should, too?"

"It's not physical, Opie. It's emotional. I think Daddy wanted to look up to his father. We can't begin to understand disappointment on that level. He's never let any of us down. I only want to help them have a future relationship."

Opie massaged the sudden pain in her forehead. "I suppose we need to give Daddy the emotional support he needs to confront his demon."

"Don't call him a demon," Val said.

She sighed. "You know what I mean."

"This is important. I have this feeling Daddy's happiness hinges on forgiving Grandfather."

Hadn't she recently told Wendell he needed to forgive, as well? Opie yawned. "Don't be disappointed if things don't turn out as you expect."

"Wouldn't it be wonderful if they connected?"

"That only happens in movies and books," Opie said.

"I know, but whatever happens, we have God by our side."

"Amen to that. See you later. I need sleep."

A few minutes later, Opie lay on her bed, her mind spinning as she tried to sort out the wild tangle of emotions. She wasn't convinced their visit would serve a positive purpose but would go for her father's sake. The idea that they were about to awake a furor that might never be silenced wouldn't go away.

Eventually she slept and rose when the alarm went off to dress for her event. Her mother worked in the kitchen. Sammy came running, holding up a paper plate mask to her face. "Oh, you frightened me." Opie gasped and the child giggled in delight. After admiring Sammy's coloring, she took a bottle of water from the fridge. "Mom, what do you think about us visiting grandfather?"

Mom rinsed the potatoes and turned off the water. She reached for the potato peeler. "I think Val could be right. Your dad hasn't visited Mathias in years."

"Did you ever meet him?"

"Once. Your dad took Val and the twins to meet his father. It didn't go well, and after that Jacob insisted we keep that part of his life separate."

Opie couldn't believe what she was hearing. "Is that really possible?"

"I respected his feelings and tried not to interfere."

She drank from the bottle and twisted the cap back on. "You never felt God wanted you to do anything?"

Her mother rinsed the potatoes again and dumped them into a pot. "I'm sensitive to what this does to your dad. I listen and we talk. When he's upset, I pray with him. I've prayed for Mathias as well."

"Has Dad said how he feels about this trip?"

Mom chuckled. "You mean other than he'd rather be hit in the head with a sledgehammer?"

Her dad always said that about things he didn't like doing. Opie hugged her mom. "Gotta run. I'll be late tonight."

She paused to say bye to Sammy and rushed off, her thoughts turning to the job she was about to do.

eleven

By the end of the night, Opie felt as if someone had taken a snuffer to her double-ended candle. She welcomed the break in her schedule and looked forward to time for herself. Later that morning, she took a walk out into the gardens and decided to call Wendell. She hadn't seen him at the parties she'd done for his friends and wanted to thank him for recommending her. Unsure whether he was home or away on business, she dialed his cell phone.

They talked for a few minutes before he said, "Have lunch with me on Saturday."

Opie knew her schedule was clear. "What did you have in mind?"

"A surprise."

She found that curious. Wendell Hunter didn't strike her as a man who cared for surprises.

"Okay. What time?"

"I'll pick you up around ten."

"What should I wear?"

"Dressy casual."

The conversation ended, and Opie shut off her cell phone and puzzled over the invitation. After all this time, why would he invite her to lunch? They hadn't spoken since the engagement party. She was no closer to an answer when he arrived Saturday morning.

"You look really nice," Wendell said when she greeted him at the door.

Opie thought him very handsome in his navy blazer and khaki slacks. "Thanks." She opted for a black pantsuit with a lacy purple top underneath, hoping it would be okay for their destination. She'd added a pair of wedge heels.

"I was surprised that you called," Wendell said.

His words seemed tentative. Opie didn't tell him she'd been equally surprised when he invited her to lunch. "I wanted to thank you. I've been so busy I haven't had the opportunity until now. You haven't been at the parties," she offered, almost an accusation.

"I've been traveling for business."

Opie knew the farm wasn't his only business interest. She felt hopeful they'd get past that last uncomfortable session.

Even if they could never be more than friends, she needed to be part of his life.

When they approached Keeneland, Opie instinctively knew this was Wendell's surprise. She'd never set foot inside the gates of the national historic landmark Thoroughbred horseracing and sales facility. She'd seen photos of the limestone buildings and the well designed, meticulous landscaping and read articles extolling the traditions of the track founded by Jack Keene in 1935 on 147 acres of farmland west of Lexington. From its onset, Keeneland used proceeds from the spring and fall live races and auctions to further the Thoroughbred industry and contribute back to the community.

"Hunter Farm has a couple of horses running today, and I hoped you might help me cheer them on to victory," Wendell said.

He made it difficult to say no. Opie told herself it was only lunch, but her desire to witness his world warred against her dad's displeasure. Wendell won. "I've never been here before."

People filled the area. As with other sports, tailgaters had set up beneath the glorious red and gold trees in the parking lot.

"Jacob was probably here last month for the yearling sales," Wendell commented as they entered.

Opie didn't know. He never mentioned the tracks. "It's possible."

Wendell slowed his stride to match hers. "You'd probably like to visit the kitchens. We should have come for breakfast at the Track Kitchen and watched the horses work out this morning." He stopped walking and asked, "Is something wrong? You're awfully quiet."

Sensory overload from trying to take in too much too fast, Opie thought. "No, I'm fine." She'd worry about how to explain this to her dad later.

Even she knew this wasn't a typical sightseeing experience. Wendell gave her a complete tour of the area before he said, "Let's eat, and then we can check out the horses prior to post time. We're having lunch in the clubhouse."

Opie admired the beautifully set up buffet luncheon in the clubhouse but could barely recall what she'd eaten. She saw a different side of Wendell as he talked horses with the other owners and trainers. He confidently advised them he was there to win today and spirited disputes rose up over the race outcome. In the end, they wished each other the best of luck.

Eventually they made it down to the paddock. The area swarmed with people. Owners, trainers, and jockeys viewed the competition and received last-minute advice while fans admired the beautiful horses and made their picks for the winner. The beautiful hats drew Opie's attention. She'd never been able to keep them on her head and often wished she could wear them as well as these women did.

Wendell introduced her to his trainer, Terrence Malone. Opie stood by while they discussed the upcoming races.

"I have a good feeling about today, Mr. Hunter."

Wendell nodded and glanced at the jockey who wore the Hunter Farm silks. "What about you, Dan?"

"Dell Air's the one to beat today, sir. There he is."

Opie's gaze turned to the impressive gray Thoroughbred. It was the first time she'd seen Wendell's colt. Standing at almost seventeen hands, Dell Air's sleek muscles rippled beneath his well-groomed coat. Opie experienced the eeriest feeling that Dell Air knew he was on display. She would almost say he posed for those who watched.

A few minutes later, the trainer gave Dan a leg up.

They arrived back at their seats just before the call-to-post bugle. Opie felt the crowd's excitement when the horses came out onto the track to parade before the grandstand before they moved toward the gate. Wendell pointed to Dell Air, and breathless anticipation filled her as the horses rocketed from the gates and down the track. Soon the jockeys rode so low all she could see was the color of their caps. The gray hugged the inside, moving through the ranks and to the front and was soon neck and neck with the leader. In the last few seconds, he pulled ahead and won the race.

Opie hadn't realized she'd been yelling encouragement until Wendell chuckled. She couldn't take her eyes off his smiling face when they declared his colt the winner. Wendell swung her up and around, and then he kissed her. "I should bring you along for good luck every time," he declared.

She touched her lips, struggling to understand what had just happened.

"Come on," Wendell said, grabbing her hand.

"No. You go ahead. I need to visit the ladies room."

Wendell looked confused. "Are you sure?"

Opie nodded. Not only did she need time alone, but also there was no place for her in the winner's circle among the photographers and media. "I'll meet you back here."

She stood before the bathroom mirror for some time, reliving the touch of his lips against hers. *It was the excitement,* she thought. The gesture hadn't meant anything to him. Unfortunately, it meant too much to her.

Jubilant upon his return, Wendell placed the ticket in her hand, "Here's a little gift for you."

Opie saw it was for the race Dell Air had just won. "No. I couldn't," she said, pushing it back at him.

Wendell frowned. "I bought it for you."

"I can't."

His mouth thinned with his displeasure. "Your sister took her winnings."

"Val worked hard on her project. The gift was her bonus. I haven't done anything."

"Sure you have. You've done a stellar job this summer. Here, take it."

She shook her head and stepped back. "I can't, Wendell. I'm sorry."

Tension stretched between them. "What's going on, Ophelia? You wouldn't go to the winner's circle, and now you're refusing my gift."

Would he understand if she told him she'd been overcome by her emotions after the kiss or that she hadn't wanted to risk her family seeing her on television? The furtiveness of this outing weighed heavy on her heart.

He seemed disappointed at her hesitation. "You want to leave?"

Opie considered his question and nodded. "I'll call someone to pick me up. I don't want to take you away from the races."

"I brought you here. I'll take you home."

A less talkative Wendell escorted her to the car. Silence stretched as he drove toward home. Finally he spoke. "What's going on in your head, Ophelia?"

"I shouldn't have gone." She sensed his immediate withdrawal. "You don't need to feel guilty. It was my decision. I could have refused, but I wanted to see for myself."

"It's business, Ophelia. I can't keep barns of horses for pleasure. They have to pay for themselves."

"I know."

"Why is your family so against racing?"

"I told you before Wendell. It's the temptation. Daddy will be upset when I tell him."

"You're a grown woman, Ophelia. Your father doesn't control your actions."

"No, but my love and respect for him does," she said.

"I don't get it," Wendell said. "He supports his family breeding Thoroughbreds. And you said he doesn't have a problem."

Opie knew Wendell needed to hear the whole story. "My grandfather did." Her voice lowered as she said, "He killed a man over a petty bet in a drunken brawl. He's serving a life sentence and has been in prison since my dad was seventeen years old."

He took in a sharp, quick breath. "I'm sorry, Ophelia. I thought we could have a fun outing. It never occurred to me that your family was dealing with something of that magnitude."

Opie knew she needed to tell her family what she'd done but was glad no one asked where she'd been. She could still see Wendell's expression when she'd told him about her grandfather. Had she imagined his reaction? She didn't think so.

A few days later, the trip to Eddyville was history and as Opie suspected, neither father nor son greeted each other with open arms.

She could definitely see her dad in Mathias Truelove's outer self, but they were nothing alike. Her dad hadn't been happy. In fact, he'd been almost disrespectful to his father. That surprised Opie. If anything, she expected him to treat his dad with respect.

Opie appreciated the way Val controlled the visit, asking their father and grandfather not to argue and even defending her when Mathias commented that she was goofing off and could easily find a job if she was any good. When he brought up the lottery win, Val maintained that it was a gift from God. He'd been critical of their beliefs, but they assured him there was nothing wrong with serving the Lord. He asked his son if he still ran that farm, and no one mentioned the change of ownership. Their dad insisted they keep their personal business to themselves.

One point stuck in Opie's head. Even after thirty years in prison, her grandfather's fondest memories weren't of his family but of racing. "Going to the tracks always got my heart pumping," he'd said with a laugh. "There were days when I got so close to a big win that I thought I'd die right there of a heart attack."

After witnessing his exhilaration, Opie compared her reaction. She'd experienced the excitement in terms of seeing the horses run. Like any sports fan, she'd rooted for her horse and found satisfaction in Dell Air's victory. But when it came to memories, her first kiss from Wendell scored much higher.

Opie definitely understood Val's concerns when she witnessed her dad's strong reaction after they left the prison. Jacob admitted he'd tried to forgive his father but couldn't. His harsh comment that every man in the prison deserved to be there made Val ask if he'd love them any less if they made wrong decisions. Even though he'd said he wouldn't, Opie couldn't help but think how disappointed he would be when she told him what she'd done. She knew that only God could heal the father-son relationship.

After a restless night, Opie felt she wouldn't find peace until she told her dad the truth. Wendell might not understand why they avoided temptation, but she learned a valuable lesson. After hearing her grandfather yesterday, she knew why her dad felt as he did.

Opie went to find Jacob. She found him watching the exercise boys breeze the yearling they'd recently acquired. She remembered innocently asking what that meant once. Her father had gone into detail about the training method where the horses ran at more than a fast gallop over varying track lengths. There had been more, but she'd zoned out and missed that part. *Had this colt come from the Keeneland sales?* Opie wondered.

Jacob spoke to the trainer before he turned to her. "Is something wrong?"

Opie understood why he'd think that. She rarely searched him up on his turf. She should come back when he wasn't busy. "I can wait."

"Not if it's important enough to bring you out here now."

She couldn't look him in the eye as she said, "I went to the track with Wendell last Saturday." He didn't say anything, and she hurriedly explained, "He invited me to lunch. I didn't know we were going to Keeneland. Dell Air won."

Jacob started walking back to the farm office. Opie walked beside him. "Wendell has high hopes for that horse. Did you place a bet?"

"No," Opie said with an emphatic shake of her head. "Wendell tried to give me a winning ticket after the race and got upset when I turned him down. He brought up Val's winnings. I tried to explain the difference. While they were both gifts, this seemed more like ill-gotten gains."

"Conscience?" her dad asked.

"Exactly," Opie agree with a barely perceptible dip of her head. "I told myself it would be okay so long as I didn't gamble."

"People don't always understand others' values. What did you hope to find out by going?"

Her father's calm handling of the situation made things harder. She almost wished he would yell or shout. "I should have said no, but I wanted to see for myself. I guess I wanted it to not be what you've always told us."

His eyebrows slanted in a frown. "Why?"

"Because of Wendell." Her voice broke miserably with the admission.

"You care for him?"

She nodded. "He calls himself an old sinner and says he's not good for me. I know I'll never have more than his friendship."

"He's given your business a leg up," Jacob said. "You know, Opie, I can only ask you kids not to do things and give you what I hope are good reasons as to why it's a bad idea, but ultimately God gave you freedom of choice. Each of you has to decide what's right and wrong.

"What you witnessed Saturday is Bluegrass tradition. The Sport of Kings," he emphasized. "Millions of dollars change hands at the tracks. The majority of people there hope to put a substantial portion in their bank account. Some will go home content with a fun outing, but others will suffer major disappointment."

He stopped and looked at her. "Your mom and I have been blessed not to see our children in trouble over the years, and I believe it's because God has been a shining light in your decision-making process. I know each of you asks what Jesus would do."

Opie couldn't say she'd done that this time. The urge to see

Wendell in his environment pushed the thought right out of her head. "I felt guilty because I knew you'd be disappointed."

"Conscience will get you every time," Jacob agreed with a crooked smile. "All my father cared about was a good time, and in the end it became his downfall. He wasted his life and money.

"We were in the courtroom the day they found him guilty. He refused to accept the blame for his actions. If he got drunk, it was the bartender's fault. If he lost his money, it was the horse's fault. He claimed the man picked a fight and yet rather than walk away, he made a choice that cost a man his life and him his freedom.

"That's why I've always talked about accepting the consequences of your decisions. I will say he was role model enough to show me that I never wanted that kind of life for my children. I've been a tough taskmaster, but I do what I do out of love. I may not tell you enough, but I love you. I'd willingly give up everything, including my life, for you."

Choked with emotion, Opie nodded.

"Wendell feels the need to prove himself worthy of being his father's son."

"You should have seen him in the clubhouse. He was in his element."

"He's spent the last ten years of his life doing that."

"He says the horses have to pay for themselves," Opie said. "How will we survive without that income?"

"God will show us the way."

"Will buying and selling horses be enough?"

"We're looking at other ways of raising capital."

"Yet another reason I should make a decision about my future and be less of a drain on the family budget," Opie said as they walked on. "I'll let you get back to work. I needed to get this off my chest. I'm sorry, Daddy."

"Don't be sorry, Opie. I appreciate your honesty. Learning the truth from another source would have hurt more."

"I know. I never meant to hurt you, Daddy. I just wanted

to see for myself. Did you know they feed thousands of people there every day?"

He nodded. "I've eaten breakfast at the Track Kitchen when I go for the sales."

"Wendell mentioned that place."

Her dad chuckled. "Leave it to you to go to Keeneland and come home thinking about food."

Opie smiled at his teasing remark. "Do I need to tell the others?"

"Only if you want to. As far as I'm concerned, it's between you and God."

She hugged him. "Forgive me?"

"There's nothing to forgive, Opie. I won't promise not to try to convince you not to follow your heart, but I do promise to be there for you whatever the outcome."

twelve

The sun shone brightly on a crisp early November day as the Truelove family prepared for the arrival of their guests. Opie and her siblings enjoyed surprising their parents with breakfast in bed.

"I have horses to attend to," Jacob argued when they settled the tray across his lap.

"Not today." Opie tucked a cloth napkin into the neck of his pajama top. "It's an official holiday on the property. No horses on Cindy Day."

Her mother laughed. "I take it you couldn't get the mayor to make it official in Paris?"

"We tried, but he couldn't see his way clear to grant our request. Something about others wanting their own official day," Val declared with a frown. "Sorry, Mom, no key to the city."

"Here at home will do just fine," Mom assured with a chuckle.

Opie removed the domed cover to reveal all her mother's breakfast favorites. "We want you to take it easy today. The guest rooms are ready for your sisters, Grammy, Uncle Zeb, and Jen. Aunt Karen couldn't make it." Opie looked forward to seeing her cousin, Jennifer. They became close when she lived with them while attending culinary school.

"When do their flights get in?"

"Everything's handled," Heath said. "A limo will transport them to the farm in style."

"They will think we've gone crazy," Mom said.

"Not until later," Val said, sharing a grin with her siblings.

"Valentine," her mother asked, "what are you planning?"

"It's a surprise, Mom. Don't worry. You're going to have the time of your life."

"I suppose as long as you didn't bring the circus to town," she muttered uneasily.

"Oh, you don't like the circus?" Val asked with mock concern.

Opie giggled at her startled expression.

"She's pulling your leg, Mom," Rom said.

"Spoilsport," Val called, nudging him with her shoulder.

After a few minutes, Opie left them to enjoy their breakfast. Her role for the day was a busy one. There were plans for breakfast, a barbecue luncheon for two hundred guests, and a sit-down dinner. Any one event would have been enough for their mother, but they wanted to ensure that everyone who mattered to her had the opportunity to celebrate her birthday. Breakfast was for their parents; lunch for church, community friends, and family; and dinner for family and close friends.

Opie took a few minutes around two to fix herself a plate. She enjoyed the succulent barbecue as she watched the this-is-your-life large screen presentation Jules put together with photos of her mom from birth to present including interviews with their dad, her children, siblings, and friends. When Cindy Truelove smiled at the newborn in her arms—probably Cy given the more current hairstyle—Opie accepted her mother had exactly what she'd always wanted.

All this time, she'd thought her mother needed more to be fulfilled when in reality her children were the woman's finest creations. She might spend hours putting a delectable meal on the table, but what did she have after it was eaten? A few compliments and maybe more work. Food couldn't love her back like a family. Couldn't be there for her in the future when she was elderly and retired from a career that would probably give her ulcers and turn her hair gray.

Opie continued to mull this over as she visited with their guests for a while and then went back to the kitchen to prepare the rack of lamb for their sit-down dinner. A second birthday cake layered three levels high and covered with the delicate pastel sugar flowers she'd spent hours making by hand sat on the sideboard in the dining room.

Her catering assistants' familiarity with her work methods made things go smoothly. The servers ensured their guests had everything they needed. At six, Opie checked one last time to be sure the rooms were set up properly. Tables from the tent would seat the guests who did not fit around the dining table.

The fantasy took her breath away. Candles flickered in their antique holders, beautiful linens draped the tables, and their mother's favorite roses filled the crystal vases throughout the room. A small gift commemorating the event sat at each place. Never in all her wildest imagining would Opie have thought they would host such a party.

She exchanged her chef whites for the lavender silk maxidress she'd chosen for the event. She could hardly wait to see the others in their formal wear. No doubt her parents had been surprised to find the new formal dress and tux laid out on the bed in their room.

After appetizers in the drawing room, Val said, "Everyone find your place cards and have a seat."

Opie hadn't noticed the cards earlier. When she stepped into the room, Wendell tipped his head to indicate the chair next to him. He stood and watched her approach. "You're looking particularly beautiful tonight."

The open admiration in his expression nearly left Opie speechless. "Thank you," she managed after getting herself seated.

"I hope you don't mind that I'm here."

Memories of their times together filled her head. "How have you been?"

"Busy. I owe you an apology."

"No," she said sharply. "Let's don't talk about that."

"But. . ."

"Wendell, please don't," she said softly, smiling at her aunts and cousin Jennifer when they joined them. She introduced him as their friend and neighbor. Mostly thanks to her aunts, the conversation flowed throughout the meal. Opie contributed, but her attention focused on the servers.

"Relax. They have everything under control," Wendell whispered in her ear.

"I know. I just want it to be perfect."

His gaze lingered on her face. "It is."

Tears came to her eyes when her tuxedo-clad father presented his wife with a diamond cross necklace. The love in their expressions spoke volumes as he brushed aside her hair and fastened the necklace before kissing her. Wendell caught her hand underneath the table and squeezed comfortingly.

"It's all too much," her teary-eyed mom protested.

"It can never be enough," her dad countered.

The dinner concluded with her mother blowing out her candles and everyone singing "Happy Birthday." Her aunts went off to visit with their sister.

"Opie, the food was spectacular," her grandmother Truelove enthused when her son escorted her from the dining room. "You children did your mother proud."

"Thanks, Grammy." Opie stood and hugged her.

"When are you coming to see me again? I've missed those special dishes you prepared."

She'd often prepared meals for her aunt's family and took food over to her grandmother when she lived in Florida. "I've missed you, too."

"She tells me I should go to culinary school," Jen told her. "I tell her I can barely boil water."

Opie chuckled. She knew that to be a fact. Her attempts to interest her cousin in cooking had been a major flop.

"I'm so happy you came," she said, squeezing Jen's shoulder and sliding her arm about her grandmother's waist. "You're staying through tomorrow, I hope."

"We don't fly out until late Monday afternoon," Jen said. "Uncle Jacob said he'd give me a tour of the farm after church tomorrow."

"Val suggested I spend more time here at the farm with

your family," Lena Truelove said. "I told her perhaps when the weather is warmer."

"Put us on your schedule for next August for sure. We're already planning Dad's birthday event for next year."

"No way," Jacob declared. "I want to celebrate my birthday just like we did this year."

"Horse kick and all?"

"Now that part we can skip. My family, friends, and favorite foods are all I ever want."

"This has been fun, Jacob," his mother said. "I'm looking forward to seeing what you plan for Cindy next year to top this."

Opie laughed at her father's helpless look. "Don't worry, Daddy. We plan to come up with lots of reasons for you to wear that tux."

They chuckled when he tugged at the collar of his shirt and said, "I was afraid of that."

After they moved on, she dropped back into her chair.

"How are you doing?" Wendell asked. "From all accounts, you've done a marathon food service today."

"Tired but happy," Opie told him. "I wasn't sure I could pull it off."

Wendell smiled. "But you did."

The photographer they'd hired to capture the memories of the day came by and asked Wendell to move closer. He placed his arm about the back of her chair. His warmth radiated through her.

She'd steered clear of him lately, not wanting to embarrass him or herself further. Wendell seemed to have the same intention.

"I saw you and Russ talking earlier," she commented after the photographer left. "Everything okay?"

Wendell looked briefly over his shoulder in his brother's direction. "He wants to talk."

"I told Val what you told me," Opie admitted. "She told him this afternoon."

Wendell didn't say how he felt about what she'd done, but

Opie thought Russ needed to know the truth.

"We'll see what happens. What else have you been doing?"

"Mostly working. Your friends have kept me busy with the parties. And we visited my grandfather in prison."

Wendell's brows rose. "How did that go?"

"Pretty much as expected. Daddy didn't want to be there. Val feels sorry for Grandfather. She says he doesn't have any reason to change if his family doesn't care for him."

"She's got a point. But people can't always be what other people expect."

Opie knew he referred to the times she'd challenged his choices. "I owe you an apology, Wendell."

"No, you don't. Even if we don't always agree, I like that you care about your friends, Ophelia."

❧

When Russ indicated his desire to talk, Wendell suggested he come to the house the next day. He'd had no idea what was on his mind until Ophelia told him what she'd done. He wondered if they'd be able to communicate without blowing up at each other. Only time would tell. The hurt surely wouldn't go away overnight. His brother arrived right on time.

"Come into the drawing room," Wendell invited.

Russ chose the sofa and Wendell the armchair. "Why didn't you tell me about the farm?"

"I would have if you hadn't run off before I could."

When Russ would have protested, he shrugged and said, "You're right. I never gave you an opportunity." After a brief pause, he added, "I always felt you didn't like me."

Wendell decided not to sugarcoat the situation. "It wasn't you. I didn't like what you meant to Dad. I was three when my mother died. At a time when he could have taken a more active role in my life, he met your mother. He didn't have time for me after that."

"I'm sure he didn't mean. . ."

"I felt abandoned. First by my mother and then my father."

"Mom tried to love you," Russ defended.

Wendell supposed Russ would see it that way. He'd been a surly withdrawn kid for most of his brother's childhood. He could tell him the truth, but he wouldn't do that to Russ. "I suppose she did in her own way, but she loved my father and you more. She was more than happy to agree with Dad when he suggested boarding school. I needed a home with real parents. Not some institution that cared more about education than the child they were teaching."

"I'm sorry, Wendell. I didn't understand."

"You were a child. You got a bad deal, too," he admitted grudgingly. "Your mom didn't object when Dad shipped you off later."

"I don't suppose he would have listened if she had. He had only one thing on his mind—horses."

"Hunter Farm and horses," Wendell corrected.

A crease formed between Russ's brows. "How do you suppose he felt knowing the farm would never be his?"

Wendell sat with his elbow propped on the chair arm, his head resting against his hand. "He made his mark on the racing world. There's more than one trophy with him as owner/breeder. I suppose he thought that if he had to keep the farm for me, he might as well prosper, too. You know, as far as the outside world knew, it was his farm. My mother changed the name after they were married. I guess she wanted to prove she was dedicated to their future."

"And yet she left it to you?"

He shrugged. "She didn't have a choice. This land has been in her family for years. My grandfather wasn't about to risk losing it to our dad. I don't think the two of them got along very well. He opposed my mother marrying him. And even though he legally tied her hands against giving the farm to Dad, she could call it whatever she wanted."

"So she salvaged Dad's pride, and he told us it was a man's job to provide for his family."

Wendell's brow rose at Russ's comment. "He did say that often, didn't he?"

Russ nodded. "I wonder what else he hid from us."

"He was what he was, Russ. Maybe he wasn't the greatest, most understanding father, but he provided well for us. I worked with him in those last years, and I'd be the first to tell you the man knew his business when it came to horses."

"But it was always business for him. I think the Trueloves have the best attitude about their farm. They don't put it ahead of everything else."

"Like Dad did with family?" Wendell asked.

Russ nodded.

"So you plan to marry Val Truelove?"

"In time. If she'll have me."

That surprised Wendell. "Why wouldn't she?"

"Surely you know they're a very religious family."

Wendell rose to his feet and walked over to pour himself a glass of water. He held the pitcher up and Russ nodded. After handing his brother the glass, he sat back down. "Yes. Ophelia made sure I'm aware of that."

Russ chuckled. "Opie hates being called by her full name."

"She's a beautiful young woman. Not at all suited to a tomboy name like Opie."

"Do you know why they all have nicknames?"

Wendell nodded. "Ophelia told me." He took another sip of water. "So when's the wedding?"

"I haven't proposed. We only agreed last night to pursue a future together."

"That's not a proposal?" Wendell asked, puzzled by the reference.

"It's a courtship. I need to develop my relationship with God before we take any further steps."

Wendell laughed. "She's got you in church?"

"It was my decision," Russ defended. "I've been miserable for a very long time. Lonely, depressed, and determined to show you I didn't need you, either. A rash of problems with Val's project made her doubt me. I didn't like it. Rom's been living at my condo and helped me understand the real reason for my unhappiness."

"You think religion is the answer?"

"I know it is," Russ answered confidently. "I'm tired of going it alone. God has filled the void left by the loss of my parents and sent someone for me to love. He's even enabled me to seek your forgiveness."

"Does she love you?"

Russ nodded. "She's the reason I'm here. She asked me to make peace with you. They're big believers in family. I owe you an apology, Wendell. I hope you'll forgive me. When I have children, I'd like them to know their uncle. It's not as if we have a great deal of family."

"You won't be able to say that if you marry into the Truelove family."

Russ grinned and said, "That's the best part. They're a great group."

"They are," Wendell agreed. Each time he'd been in their presence, he'd come away with a feeling he couldn't quite describe—a warmth that reached deep inside and made him crave more. "Quite accomplished. How are you going to handle your wife's wealth?"

"I won't let the money come between us like it did you and me."

Wendell eyed him speculatively. "Do you think it was only the money, Russ?"

"No. It was my attitude," he admitted, adding with a grin, "and your stubbornness. I made a wrong assumption. I regret that most of all. Dad and Mom looked out for me. They left me sufficient funds to finish school and establish myself. If I'd been more mature when I lost them, I might have realized how blessed I was not to have inherited the farm." He pointed to the piano. "Do you still play?"

Wendell nodded. "Occasionally."

"I'm sure you've only gotten better over the years. Do you regret not becoming a concert pianist?"

"No. I didn't want to travel and wasn't one to enjoy the acclaim."

"I'd love to hear you play again."

"Perhaps we can get together for dinner soon."

Russ nodded. "I'm serious about us, Wendell. I'm sorry for the selfish way I shoved you from my life."

"You were a kid, Russ."

"Old enough to try to understand. I'm sorry for being such a pain as a brother."

"I resented you far too much for us to have been closer," Wendell admitted. "Perhaps we can put the past behind us and look forward to a future as friends."

"Closer than friends, I hope. I want what Val has with her siblings."

"You have high hopes for us, brother."

"Very high. I'd better get back to Val. I know she's waiting to hear the outcome."

"You think she thought I'd kick you out?"

Russ stood and shrugged. "I might have considered it if I'd been you."

"If you can be man enough to apologize, I can be man enough to accept," Wendell said, holding out his hand. Russ pulled him into a hug, and Wendell silently thanked Ophelia for her interference.

thirteen

Opie could never remember a bad holiday, and this year had been no exception. She'd accepted a number of catering jobs and private chef services for dinner parties straight through the New Year. She also found time to help prepare special meals at the homeless shelter and collect gifts for the people who attended.

She ran into Wendell occasionally. The first time, he thanked her for what she'd done for him and Russ. She'd felt a little envious when Val attended a dinner party at Wendell's home. No doubt he was interested in getting to know the woman who could become his future sister-in-law.

Wendell wasn't the only one getting a new sister-in-law. Heath surprised Jane with his Christmas Eve proposal. Opie would never have guessed Heath had that much romance in him.

The Hunters and Trueloves spent the holidays together. After Christmas dinner, Opie watched Wendell across the room and wished things could be different. He caught her watching him and concluded his conversation, rising from the chair and pausing to pick up a gift from underneath the tree.

"I bought you something."

"You shouldn't have. I didn't get you anything," Opie said. Actually, she'd sent him the same homemade cookies she'd made to thank her clients and promote her business.

"Didn't expect you to. Open it."

The gift surprised her. He'd gone to the trouble of having her name embroidered on a chef's jacket. "Oh, thank you. You shouldn't have."

"It's to replace the one you ruined at my house. And I thought it would be good advertising to have your name right there on your coat where everyone can see it."

He rambled on, explaining the gift. Opie fingered the material, finding it nicer than anything she'd buy for herself. "I'll save this one for special occasions. Thank you."

"You're welcome. Russ and I appreciate the invitation to dinner."

Opie busied herself with folding the tissue back and putting the lid back on the box. "Get used to it. Now that Val and Russ are together, you'll be treated as family."

"I can handle that," Wendell said with a wide grin.

❧

Opie made it through all the Christmas and New Year bookings and looked forward to a short break before their church choir started preparing for the Easter cantata. The cold symptoms started right after New Year's. She visited the drugstore, but the over-the-counter medicines didn't help. As she sniffled and sneezed her way through multiple boxes of tissues, she felt thankful that it hadn't affected her holiday business. Her bank account showed a tidy sum.

She kept her distance at the Sunday afternoon choir practice, not wanting to share her bounty of cold germs.

"I'm sorry, but I can't commit to playing the piano for this year's cantata," Sue Kelly announced after they listened to the Easter program. "Our tax business is picking up, and it looks as though I'm going to have to work overtime."

Sighs followed her announcement. With the downturn in the economy, no one could blame the couple for going after all the business they could get. Unfortunately, their regular pianist fell and broke her hip before Christmas. Their director Dean had carpal tunnel surgery a couple of weeks before. Things weren't looking so good for their Easter program.

"I have an idea." Everyone's attention turned to Opie. "I know this guy who is tremendously talented. He could be a concert pianist. But he's not a believer."

"I'm okay with that," Dean said. "The music and narrative in this program is so awesome that I feel it's going to touch a number of hearts, perhaps even this man."

She coughed, blew her nose, and muttered a sorry. "So it's okay if I ask?"

"Definitely. I'll get a book and CD for you to share with him."

"I don't know that he'll agree," Opie warned. "It can't hurt to ask."

After they prayed, the group called their good nights and headed for the parking lot. The twins ran on ahead and unlocked the car. Val and Opie climbed into the backseat, and Val reached for her seat belt before she said, "You're going to ask Wendell, aren't you?"

"He's fantastic, Val," she enthused. "You've heard him play. His talent is incredible, truly God-given."

Heath started the vehicle and waited for the defroster to clear the ice from the windows. He looked at her in the rearview mirror and said, "I'd like to know how you think you're going to convince a non-Christian to play for a church cantata."

"You know Opie," Rom said to his brother. "She'd take on the devil for one of her causes."

"I would not." She'd be the first to admit she didn't know how she'd get Wendell to agree, but it wouldn't happen if she didn't try. "I'll ask. If he says yes, we'll have the best cantata ever."

"I can't believe Mrs. Keaton, Sue, and Dean are all out of commission at the same time," Val said.

"Could be God at work. If I can get Wendell to the church, God can do the rest."

"It's not just a way to spend more time with him?" Val inquired softly as the twins carried on a conversation up front.

While Opie couldn't deny the fact with certainty, she'd given the matter over to God. Her feelings for Wendell were strong, and the initial challenge of convincing him to accept her as she was gave way to helping him find the Lord.

Opie didn't agree with Wendell's belief he was too old and cynical for her. She found much to admire about him, but there were times when she wished she'd never met him. If she'd known how quickly her attraction would grow out of control, she'd have steered clear of the bachelor auction that had put him in her life.

"I know it seems very unlikely that he will say yes, but if he does agree, it's a way of salvaging our cantata. You know the orchestra wants to perform, and they can't without a pianist."

"Don't get your hopes up, Opie," Val said. "Wendell's piano skills go far beyond a simple Easter program."

Opie agreed. "He's so blasé about his talent."

"Would you like for me to see if Russ will ask him?"

She considered the merits of the idea. Would Russ and Wendell's renewed relationship make him more willing to say yes? Opie doubted it. Besides, it wasn't fair to Russ. "No, but thanks."

"Have you decided how you're going to do this?"

Opie laughed and ticked off the three-point plan on her fingers. "I pray, ask, and when he says no, I beg."

❧

Wendell wondered what was on Ophelia's mind. He'd given her his cell number the night of the bachelor auction, and Ophelia didn't hesitate to contact him. So far she'd called to ask about his hands, Jean-Pierre's grandmother, thank him for the job referrals, and a couple of times just to say hello.

He liked Ophelia. A lot. If he let her, she'd get under his skin. Wendell was a realist. He knew he wasn't the man for Ophelia Truelove. He cared about her enough to stay away from her idealistic beliefs. They clashed badly enough on their fundamental beliefs of what a wife and home entailed. But he did admit to missing her since the surprise trip to the track. He'd wanted to see how she responded to his world, and she'd done fine up until he'd kissed her and tried to foist the ticket on her.

Wendell glanced at the offending object. He hadn't even cashed it in, just brought the ticket home and tucked it into the picture frame on his desk to serve as a reminder of their differences.

The doorbell rang, and he glanced at his watch. She must have been standing by the door when she called. Knowing Opie, maybe even sitting in the car, Wendell considered with a grin.

"Hi. I brought you a present," she announced, laying the package of cookies on his desk.

His mouth watered. He'd downed the first sleeve in one sitting. His intention of eating one cookie soon become another and another until all that remained were a few crumbs in the bottom of the cellophane wrapper. "What's this? A bribe?"

She shrugged and said, "I do have a favor to ask." Ophelia rummaged through her huge purse and removed a book and CD. "Our pianists at church are out of commission, and we really need help with our Easter cantata. I hoped you might consider playing for us."

"I don't do church, Ophelia." How many times would he have to tell her he wasn't interested before she got the message?

"I know, but you do music. What if I promise no one will try to change your mind? We can create a contract. Pay you for your services. Please. We really need you."

"It wouldn't work."

She paused for a coughing spasm, the sound deep and abrasive. Opie pulled a tissue from her pocket and dabbed at her eyes. "You're the most talented pianist I've ever heard," she said, flashing him a winsome smile. "All you'd have to do is play the songs along with our orchestra. You could make our Easter program the best we've ever had."

Wendell poured her a cup of water from the pitcher on his desk. She thanked him and took a sip.

"It's a busy time of year."

"We only practice once a week."

He knew from experience that it took hours to become comfortable with the music.

"I don't think. . ."

"Please," she said, laying the book and CD before him. "At least listen. After that, if you say no, we'll try to find someone else."

"You can't find another pianist?"

"Not like you. Just think about it," she pleaded, noting his unyielding expression.

"I'm not making any promises."

"We'd only ask you to commit to playing for us until the Easter performance," she assured. "After the rave reviews, you can go your way knowing you have the undying gratitude of the choir and musicians."

"I'll let you know."

"It's a beautiful program, Wendell. Just listen and maybe play a couple of the songs."

She didn't know when to quit. "Okay," he relented. Maybe it was the eagerness of her expression or the desire to give her what she asked when it was so little. Perhaps he could carve out a few hours in his schedule. He couldn't imagine how she'd keep her promise but knowing Ophelia, she'd do everything possible to make it happen.

"I'm only saying I'll listen. Not that I'll agree to play."

"Thanks so much, Wendell."

Another wave of coughing hit her, so deep and rough that he thought it would tear her apart. "Have you seen the doctor yet?"

She sipped the water, her voice hoarse when she spoke. "I'm better. Rest, fluids, and ten days," Opie said. "That's all he'll tell me."

"Let's make a deal. You see the doctor, and I'll listen to your program and get back to you."

"Deal." The brilliance of her smile increased by megawatts. "I'd shake hands, but you don't want my germs. Our next practice is Sunday afternoon at 4:30. If you could let me know before then. Enjoy your cookies and don't worry, I didn't cough on them." All of a sudden, she seemed eager to escape.

The rest of Wendell's day didn't go as planned. The hopes he'd held for his meeting dissipated when the other party didn't see the benefits of his proposal. They agreed to a later discussion and went their separate ways. Terrence called to say he'd entered Dell Air in a number of upcoming races. At least the colt was earning his keep.

After dinner, he opted for a book and early night. On Thursday, while digging through the papers on his desk searching for car keys, he spotted the CD and remembered his promise to Ophelia. He'd listen to it on the drive to Louisville. At least then he'd be able to say he'd done as she asked when he refused her offer. He hoped she'd kept her end of the bargain and seen a doctor.

❧

Three days with no word from Wendell convinced Opie he wasn't going to agree. The thought saddened her.

Opie knew she shouldn't expect miracles when it came to Wendell Hunter. She also knew the promise that no one would try to proselytize him was unrealistic. Members of her church would share their faith despite her promise. Like an ostrich tucking its head in the sand, she'd hoped he would say yes and not ignore their message.

She'd give Wendell another day or so before calling Dean. Meanwhile, she needed to get to the doctor's office for her appointment.

❧

Wendell was hooked. He'd listened to the cantata and found himself captivated. The music and words touched him. Oh, he'd done his best to block out the feelings, but God refused to be silenced. Even now, the music and a few lines of dialogue played in his head. He hadn't looked at the book, but could all but see his fingers moving over the piano keys. Hands that played the masters itched to play this program.

A wry smile tilted his mouth. No doubt Ophelia hoped this would happen. How would she react if he agreed? Maybe he should put some outrageous spin on his acceptance. He could demand a grand piano. At least then, he could bow out gracefully when she said it wasn't possible. Or would Ophelia rush out to rent or buy one? She'd mentioned a church orchestra. He'd played with orchestras but never a church group. How good were they?

Wendell couldn't help but feel flattered by her praise. He'd written a few songs. Even once recorded a CD as a gift for his father. He doubted the old man cared about his son's piano playing, but Nicole often asked him to play for their party guests. Wendell suspected that was the only thing he did that impressed her.

That night he sat and listened again, this time uninterrupted. The surround sound from his expensive system magnified the music, and it resonated throughout the room.

He took the book to the piano and played through the one song that made the greatest impact on him. When the music seemed to flow from his fingers, Wendell continued, playing through song after song until he completed the program.

He checked the time and dialed Ophelia's cell number. "I'll do it. When do we start?"

The silence stretched on for several seconds before she spoke. "Oh, Wendell, thank you."

"What kind of piano do you have at church?" he asked, expecting to hear they had a traditional upright. He didn't really care. He'd rent his own piano if need be.

"It's a big one like yours. Only it's white."

That surprised him. Small churches rarely had grand pianos. "How big is your church, Ophelia?"

"We have about five thousand members."

The numbers didn't bother him. He'd played for many more. Still, five thousand members and only two pianists? Something didn't sound right. "When can I see the piano?"

"I'll ask Dean, our director, to give you a call and set up a time."

She grew silent and he could hear her coughing. "Sorry. We do appreciate this, Wendell."

"Did you see the doctor?"

"Yes. He gave me an antibiotic."

"Good. I suppose I need to audition?"

"Oh no," she exclaimed. "Everyone's very excited about the possibility. I'm so thankful I don't have to disappoint them."

"See you Sunday."

ॐ

Opie turned off the phone and let out a scream of joy as she raced downstairs to the drawing room. "He said yes."

Taken aback by her excitement, Val glanced at Russ and back at Opie. "Who?"

"Wendell. He just called to say he'll play for our cantata."

"Congratulations, Opie," Val said. "I didn't think you'd be able to convince him."

"I didn't. God did. I left the program music and asked him to listen. I'd pretty much given up hope until he called tonight. Only thing is I promised no one would talk to him about God."

"How will you manage that?" Val asked.

"I'll play it by ear."

"I think we should pray," Russ said. "Wendell needs to know God. Let's send up a specific prayer that he hears a message he can't reject, whether it be in the program or someone's words."

They bowed their heads and joined hands, sending up the request. Opie closed with a fervent amen.

ॐ

Wendell met with the choir director Friday afternoon. The piano was the same model he had at home.

"It was donated by a member who decided she'd rather have a black piano. The church was happy to take it off her hands."

Did people really do that? He'd never considered changing his piano to suit a decorating style. Of course, his piano was for use and not display.

"You're very talented," Dean said after Wendell played through one of the songs. "Opie said you were."

"Did you really need a pianist?" Wendell asked.

Dean held up his bandaged hand. "Carpal tunnel surgery. We've also got a broken hip and a pianist with financial needs. That's everyone in our group that plays the piano."

"You don't think anyone will be offended if you don't ask the church?" Wendell's brow lifted with the question. He knew people often felt territorial in certain environments, and he wouldn't want his presence to cause dissension.

"Based on Opie's comments, I feel we can promote you as a special gift from above. A guest musician. Of course, learning a long musical program isn't an easy task. Are you okay with that?"

"Ophelia seems to think I can handle it with one practice a week," Wendell said with a smile.

"She doesn't understand. Do you have the time?"

Wendell nodded. "I'll make time. The music hooked me the first time I heard the CD. I've already played it through."

"The whole book?" Dean asked. When Wendell nodded, he said, "We have the orchestra accompaniment here at church."

"Ophelia mentioned an orchestra. What instruments?"

"There's a good variety. Trumpet, clarinet, french horn, harp, drums, and violin."

"How good are they?"

"One or two actively pursue their music. Most have played since they were children and use their talent for the Lord."

Wendell considered his own reasons for not doing the same. The Lord didn't care for him or his talent. "When do we start?"

"Practice is on Sunday at 4:30. You're welcome to play anytime you like to get a feel for the sound. We could have used the split track, but everyone agrees its better when we have live musicians."

Wendell grinned. "You won't find a musician who would argue that point."

&

Ophelia called to invite Wendell to ride to the church with them. "I appreciate the offer, but I'll drive myself." He didn't want to be stranded if things didn't work out. No matter what Ophelia promised, he figured someone would bring up religion, and he needed to be prepared.

Later, when he parked next to the Trueloves' SUV, Opie climbed out and waited for him to exit his vehicle.

"I waited to walk in with you."

"Always a pleasure to be accompanied by a lovely lady."

"The others are inside."

"Others?"

"Russ, Val, and Heath. Rom couldn't make it this afternoon."

"They're all in the choir?"

Opie nodded.

As indicated, the choir assembled at the front of the church. Dean introduced him to the group. "This is Wendell Hunter. Opie told us he's very talented, and I must admit she did not exaggerate."

She wrinkled her nose playfully at the director.

"We'll miss Mrs. Keaton and Sue, but Mr. Hunter's ability will enable us to give our best to God."

"Please, call me Wendell."

"Okay everyone, you heard the man. Let's get started." After a brief prayer, they got serious about their music.

Wendell found the orchestration version on the piano and played through the introduction. Applause filled the sanctuary. "Keep that up and my head will be too big to get through the doors," he said with a laugh.

"Maybe Val should let us sing at the pavilion," Opie said. "Plenty of room for a big head out there."

"I'd love to have a summer performance, but for Easter I prefer the church," Dean said.

The others agreed as they took their places and opened their choral books.

There were a few mix-ups before the musicians settled into the program, but Wendell found them to be talented. The practice flew by and soon the director brought it to a close.

"You did really well tonight," Opie told Wendell. She coughed a time or two.

"You have a beautiful voice," he complimented, speaking of her solo in the program.

"You mean compared to a walrus?" she asked with a grin.

He shook his head at her teasing, and she called good night before going out to the vehicle where the others waited.

fourteen

"That cold isn't going to get any better if you don't take care of yourself," Mom said after Opie suffered through another bout of coughing. She'd finished the antibiotics, but the cold hung on.

Her mother insisted she rest, but Opie found it difficult to be idle. "I haven't worked since I got sick."

"You've spent a lot of time at the pavilion. It's cold out there."

Opie glanced around. "Where's Val?"

"She and Heath went into Lexington. He's found some stone he wanted her to see."

"He can't lay stone in the snow."

"That's what I told him, but he says he can have everything ready for when the weather changes."

"Another couple of months at least," Opie said, pulling her feet up into the chair and wrapping her arms about her legs. "It's going to be difficult to get people out to the pavilion."

"Your dad says he'll haul them out in a horse-drawn sleigh if need be. Heath says the ground is solid. He mentioned some sort of rock base that's helping keep the area from being too wet."

"That's good to know. I'm trying to come up with a special menu. Of course, it's impossible to top what Russ has in mind."

When Russ revealed his plan to propose to Val on Valentine's Day, which also happened to be her birthday, he enlisted the help of her entire family. Opie promised to get her sister out to the pavilion.

Opie planned to cater the event from the pavilion's lower floor kitchen. She cleared her schedule for the week. Nothing would stand in the way of doing this for Val.

"If you don't get better, you'll spend Valentine's Day in bed."

"Okay, Mom. I get the message. It's just that there are so

many details to be worked out."

Her cell rang, and Opie fished it out of her robe pocket.

"Russ tells me your cold's worse."

"Hello, Wendell," Opie managed just before she went off into a paroxysm of coughing. "I'm doing my best to shake this thing."

"I'm sure that's what my mother thought."

Opie recalled that his mother died of pneumonia. Her heart went out to the little boy who had been deprived of his mother. "Wendell, I'll be fine," she said, smiling her thanks to her mom when she handed her the orange juice. "Did Russ fill you in on his plan?"

"He came by this morning for breakfast. Said you're cooking. Are you up to that?"

"I'll be 100 percent by then. I'm so happy for them. God is in control."

"Why would you think that?"

"Not think. Know. These things don't just happen. Heath and Jane. Val and Russ. Even you and Russ. Did you ever think that you would reconcile as you have?"

"I hoped that one day we might. I don't necessarily see that God played a role in what happened."

Opie wished she could reach through the phone and shake him. "God used two women you didn't even know existed a few months ago to relay your message to Russ. Believe what you will, but there are too many signs to deny the obvious." Her talking brought on another fit of coughing that exhausted her with its violence. "You shouldn't get me so worked up."

"You should rest and drink plenty of fluids."

Opie sipped her juice and said, "Yes, doctor. I even made chicken soup."

"Does it work?"

"Who cares? It tastes good."

"Chicken soup isn't enough if you're run-down or have an infection."

"I'll be okay," she stressed.

"Get better soon. I need you at church. You got me into this."

"Don't worry. I plan to be there."

But Opie found it difficult to keep that promise. Her cold worsened and she returned to the doctor who diagnosed walking pneumonia. He sent her home with strict orders to follow his instructions and threatened to put her in the hospital if she didn't.

She'd missed two practices when Wendell came by. He set the vase of flowers on the coffee table and dragged a chair over next to the sofa. Opie knew she looked as haggard as she felt. She hadn't washed her hair and wasn't wearing makeup. The old sweats belonged to one of the twins and had seen better days, but she was too sick to care.

"Why did you do this to yourself?" Wendell demanded.

She rested her head against the pillow. "Do what?"

"Work yourself to exhaustion. Look where your career crusade got you. You don't have anything to prove to anyone."

"You and I have a lot in common," Opie said with a derisive laugh. "Our drive to prove ourselves keeps us from backing down from the challenge. You're determined to be the winner your dad was, but from what you've told me he was better with horses than kids. I'm determined to prove I can carry through with my career choice."

"Who needs that proof?"

"My family. I've never been known for my ability to carry through. I want everyone to see I can do this. I can't dabble my way through life."

"We've already seen that. Look at the events you've handled in the past few months."

"All thanks to referrals from you."

"Only a few. Once people taste your food, they can't wait to get you into their kitchen."

She turned onto her side and pulled the throw up about her arms. "I compare myself to my siblings just as you compare yourself to your father. Why do you want to be like him?"

"Why do you want to be like them?" he asked, tilting his

head and stretching out his hands, palms up. "I have an obligation to the people at the farm, Ophelia."

"Is it the people or the trophies, Wendell?"

"Winning races is how I make my living. My father's
horses aren't going to be around forever. No one is going to
come for stud animals with mediocre showings at best."

"I'd tell you to hand it over to God, but you don't believe
He can help you."

"You don't understand. I need to win."

"I do understand. I feel driven to do something worthwhile, too."

"Not if you make yourself sick in the process."

"People get sick." She began to cough. Opie grabbed a
tissue and dabbed at her moist eyes. "You'll have to forgive me,
but I'm not up to fighting speed right now. I'm doing what
the doctor ordered—getting plenty of rest, and Mom has me
drinking fluids by the gallon."

"Please take care of yourself, Ophelia."

"Can we talk about something else? Tell me how the cantata is going."

"Dean seems pleased."

"I knew he would be. Are you enjoying the music?"

"Very much."

"I'm glad you stopped by." She drew a finger along the
flowers—a beautiful arrangement of red, pink, and white roses.
Opie wondered at the mixed symbolism of the bouquet. Had
Wendell bought them because he thought she'd like them,
or was he trying to tell her something? "These are beautiful.
Thank you."

"They reminded me of your gardens. I hoped they might
lift your spirits."

They had. More than he realized. "I'm determined to beat
this thing. You'll see. I have to get well soon. Russ is depending
on me."

৯

Wendell knew he'd come on too strong, and he knew why. He

was afraid for her. Afraid he would lose Ophelia as he'd lost his mother. Her violent coughing frightened him. His grandmother told him about his mother's weak lungs and problems from childhood. He suspected that had been why they hadn't wanted her to marry his father. They knew her life wouldn't be easy. She'd caught the cold from his father. He'd gone off to a horse race, leaving her home to recover. Within days, she'd been in critical condition. Another week later, she died.

His fear of losing Ophelia had more to do with his feelings for her. He could tell himself she was too young and he was all wrong for her, but lately that hadn't kept him from missing her and wondering what his life would be like with her by his side.

Opie had told him to turn it over to God. She'd been talking about his feeling inadequate in terms of the farm, but Wendell couldn't help but consider the possibility of doing the same with his feelings for Ophelia.

What would it be like to depend on God for the answers? He'd never considered that option. His father told him where he'd go to school and chose not to tell him about the farm, but Wendell made the decisions that really mattered. He'd worked through all the pain and doubt to find the man he had become. Though at times, like now, it felt as if he were still looking.

Maybe even more so because of Ophelia's expectations of him. She wanted him to care about others. She wanted him to know God's love. In his heart, all Wendell knew was that he wanted her in his life, and it was very unlikely that she'd ever be there.

❧

To his trained ear, the group improved with every week. Wendell honored his commitment but didn't tell his friends. But when he started refusing all Sunday afternoon invitations, they demanded to know what he was doing. Wendell only smiled and said it was personal.

His social circle wasn't religious either. Like him, his friends' interests revolved around the Paris social scene and horses. Derby season would soon be upon them, and they couldn't imagine what he was doing that he considered more important than that. Leo and Catherine were totally bewildered when his acceptance of their lunch invitations resulted in an early departure.

How did he explain that the Easter music revived feelings that drew him to music years before? He'd stopped writing after his father's death, but now he picked out notes on the piano as he scribbled on sheet music.

Ophelia's return to practice the week before the engagement party gave Wendell's heart a lift. She'd lost weight and looked pale, but to him she'd never been more beautiful. She sat on the front row, claiming it would be better if she experienced a coughing jag and had to leave the room. Even with the remnants of her cold, she had a wonderful alto voice that he could hear so much better with her sitting nearby.

"Opie, do you want to try your solo?" Dean asked.

"I suppose I should."

"You can sing from there."

She took the microphone Dean handed her and smiled at Wendell when he played the introduction. Wendell knew the exact moment that she lost herself in the music. Her eyes drifted closed, and her love for the Lord became even more evident in that moment.

fifteen

"Hello, Opie." She immediately recognized the caller as Sally from church. "A Brenda Clarke called here today looking for you. She sounded upset."

She remembered the young woman. "I'll give her a call," she said after Sally recited the number.

Before she could dial, security called from the gate. "There's a woman here to see you, Ms. Truelove."

"Send her to the house."

"She's on foot. Has little kids with her."

With the birthday-engagement party tomorrow night, this was the last thing she needed, but Opie could hardly turn them away. "Put them in a cart and bring them to the house."

"I'm sorry, Ms. Truelove," Brenda said minutes later when she met them outside. "I didn't know what else to do. It's Ronald. He's in jail."

"Oh," Opie gasped. "What happened?"

"He got into a fight."

"Was he drinking?" she asked softly, not wanting the children to overhear.

"Oh no, ma'am. He doesn't drink. Ronald's coworker introduced him to this man who guaranteed he could treble our investment. Now he's disappeared with our money. I told Ronald we couldn't afford this, but he wouldn't listen. He insisted we had to find a way to come up with the money. I don't know what to do," she worried. "We don't have money for bail."

Opie wished her dad were there. He'd know how to handle this, but he'd gone into Lexington, and she didn't know when he'd be home. Wendell immediately came to mind. "We need to talk to Wendell Hunter."

Brenda's horrified expression showed fear. "I called Ronald in sick today. He'll lose his job if they find out where he really is."

"No, he won't," Opie declared. And if he did, she'd personally ask her dad to help the young family. She reached for the twins' hands and took them inside. "Mom, this is Brenda Clarke and her children, Ronnie, Bonnie, and Shelley. Will you watch the kids until we get back?"

Her mother smiled at them and said, "I just took a batch of cookies from the oven. May I?" She held out her arms.

Brenda cautiously surrendered the infant. "I forgot to bring diapers."

Her years of experience showed as Opie's mother cuddled the little girl to her chest. "We'll be fine."

Opie called security for a driver, and Glenn arrived within minutes. The young mother was frightened and glanced back as Opie shepherded her into the truck. "They'll be fine. My mom is great with children."

Brenda twisted the handle of her purse nervously. "Ronald will be so angry with me."

Opie couldn't see that the man was doing such a great job on his own. "Could be Ronald needs to trust you more. He hasn't left you a lot of options."

Brenda didn't respond, and they arrived at Wendell's a couple of minutes later. Opie asked Glenn to wait for them. She reached for the doorbell, holding Brenda's arm for fear she would bolt. When she opened the door, Mrs. Carroll smiled at Opie and invited them to come in. She came inside with Brenda in tow and asked to see Wendell.

"He's changing to go out."

"We really need to see him," she pleaded, and the woman asked her to wait.

"Ophelia, what's happened?" Wendell asked as he came down the stairs at a brisk pace.

"We need your help." She glanced at Brenda and back at him. "This is Brenda Clarke. Her husband works for you." After he acknowledged her with a nod, Opie said, "He's been arrested. He got into a fight last night, and she doesn't have money to bail him out."

Wendell frowned. "What do you want me to do?"

"Help them," Opie declared without hesitation. She looked at Brenda and said, "Tell him what you told me."

The woman swiped at her watery eyes and revealed the truth. "His friend said they could make a lot of money fast."

"Have you talked to him?"

Brenda nodded her head. "Yes, sir. He said he lost his temper when his friend told him the guy took off with their money. Ronald lost over two thousand dollars. I told him it sounded too good to be true, but he's stubborn."

"She can't afford the bail, Wendell."

"I'll see what I can do."

"You have to help them," Opie insisted. "They have three small children who need their father at home."

He looked at Brenda. "Does Jack Pitt have your home number?"

"Yes, sir." Brenda looked down at the floor.

"Go home and wait to hear from me."

"But I need to go back to Ms. Opie's to pick up my children."

"I'll take you home and bring them back," Opie said. "Thank you, Wendell. I knew you'd know what to do."

❧

Her faith in him made him feel like a bigger man. "It's not over yet, Ophelia. Depending on what the friend decides to do, Ronald could go back to jail." He glanced at Brenda and asked, "Who is the other man?"

She obviously didn't want to tell him.

"You might as well share his name. Everyone will know once they see the effects of their fight."

She named Seth Canon, one of his stallion handlers.

"We'll get to the bottom of this. Go on home. Ophelia will bring your children," he said, looking to her for confirmation before he continued, "I'll let you know something as soon as possible."

After they left, he dialed the office and spoke to the manager.

"She called him in sick this morning."

He detected censure in Jack's tone. "The woman's scared out of her mind. Clarke probably told her to do that hoping to give them time to figure out what to do."

"Guess you were right about him."

Wendell didn't want to be right. He'd never struggled with money but he understood anger, particularly when someone cheated a man of his hard-earned money. He intended to look into this further. Just to be sure Seth Canon hadn't played a part in defrauding Ronald Clarke. "Get Clarke out and take him home. I'll stand his bond."

He called Ophelia's cell. "Let Mrs. Clarke know that Jack will bring her husband home."

❧

"Will these do for where you're taking me tonight?" Val asked as she entered Opie's room carrying a pair of boots. She wore the long-sleeved, purple jewel-toned wool dress Opie said would look nice and help ward off the winter chill.

"They're fine," Opie said. "You might as well give up, birthday girl. It's a surprise, and you're not going to get it out of me. And would you please stop moping around like you've lost your best friend?"

Val looked meaningfully at the vase of roses sitting on Opie's nightstand. "At least the man in your life remembered Valentine's Day. You should have gone out with him. You would have had more fun."

Opie walked closer and rubbed two fingers together in Val's face. "Know what this is? The world's smallest violin player. The poor-little-me act isn't working."

Val laughed. "Okay. I'll try to have fun."

"That's all I'm asking." Opie walked away and paused at the window. "Looks like someone left the pavilion lights on again."

Dropping onto the side of the bed, Val tugged on her boots. "I'll run out and turn them off while you finish dressing."

"I'll be ready by the time you get back," Opie promised before she disappeared into the bathroom."

After Val left, Opie flung off her robe and pulled on the dress she planned to wear. As she came out of the bathroom, her gaze drifted to the vase on her nightstand. Val must really be depressed if she envied her these dried-up roses.

She really should toss them but held off, hoping for one more day. If only there had been a romantic reason for the flowers. But maybe Wendell had bought them out of love. For a friend. She couldn't imagine anything better than spending Valentine's Day with the man she loved. Opie pushed the emotion away. Her day would come. Just like Val and Heath.

Opie wished she could see Val's face when she saw Russ at the pavilion. She thanked God that she'd started feeling like her old self. She'd enjoyed her part in the birthday-engagement party. Heath and Jane kept Val away from home all day while she organized the food. The rest of the family decorated the pavilion's lower floor while Russ and his friends worked on the main floor, clearing away the snow and ice and setting up for his proposal. When he came down for a coffee break, Opie said, "You're going to freeze up there tonight."

"We'll have our love to keep us warm."

She groaned. "Hate to tell you, but it's not enough. You'd better find some extra heavy-duty blankets. One of those fire pits wouldn't hurt. I'll make sure she's got her coat and gloves when she leaves the house."

"What about a couple of faux fur blankets? Think those would work?"

"I imagine you could get away with horse blankets if your proposal's romantic enough."

Russ chuckled, lifting his hand in good-bye as he went off to complete his task. "Thanks for the idea."

It pleased her dad that they managed to hide their guests' vehicles about the farm and transport them to the pavilion. Her parents, family members, and other guests waited in the lower-floor room.

Opie pulled on her coat as the doorbell rang. *Probably a last-minute* guest, she thought as she opened the door. "Wendell? Why aren't you at the pavilion?"

"I waited for you. I saw Val leave a few minutes ago."

"We'd better hurry. I don't think they'll be able to stand this cold for long."

He pulled her scarf tighter and insisted she put on her gloves, taking her arm as they navigated the snowy pathway.

Later, when Val stepped into the room, Opie knew she'd never forget the glow on her sister's face. She pushed her way through the crowd, Wendell in her wake. "Did you say yes?"

Val held up her hand to reveal her heart-shaped diamond ring. "You know I did."

"Beautiful. Good job," Opie commented, clapping her future brother-in-law on the back.

"Thanks for sending her out," Russ said.

"We weren't sure how to get you out here," Opie explained. "The lights did the trick."

"Congratulations," Wendell said, hugging Val and then his brother.

When Val asked where their parents were, Opie pointed to the far side of the room.

"Do they know?" she asked.

"Everyone knew but you," Opie teased. "They're pleased with your choice."

❧

On Easter Sunday, Wendell rose early and dressed in a dark suit. He didn't want to call attention to himself any more than necessary today. They would perform at the eleven o'clock morning service. Afterward the pastor would speak, and everyone would go home to enjoy their families and holiday meal. He and Russ would dine with the Trueloves.

He'd spread himself thin over the past month and a half with business, travel, practices, rehearsal, and preparing for the spring meet. As Ophelia said, he saw the Trueloves regularly now that Russ and Val were engaged. They'd already involved him in their planning sessions, asking him to play for their wedding. He was curious as to how Val planned to get a piano out to the pavilion, but she promised to do it if he agreed.

Ophelia had been busy as well. After getting over her cold, she'd jumped right back into her hectic schedule. Some nights when he saw her at practice, she looked so weary that he feared she would get sick again. She stubbornly insisted she could handle the work.

He rarely experienced performance jitters, but today Wendell found himself with butterflies. Everything about this experience seemed strange to him. He waited in the choir room. When the others arrived, obviously filled with the joy of worship, Wendell felt he'd missed out on something important. He couldn't blame them. The church was open to all. He was the one who decided not to come.

Soon everyone was in place. The rustlings and stirrings of the audience gave way to silence when the lights went down on the crowd. Dean gestured toward him and Wendell began to play. The orchestra joined in and the choir followed suit.

A strange emotion welled up in him—extreme happiness for their group's success. He'd spent most of his life solo, and for the first time he felt like part of the group. He caught Ophelia's gaze on him, her smile wide with pleasure. She winked and turned the page, though he noticed that she rarely looked at the book.

When she stepped forward for her solo, he accompanied her, playing softly as her pure, sweet voice sang of her love for the Lord. So many sensations hit him at once—Ophelia's glowing beauty. Her joy in serving the Lord. His love for her.

He almost stopped playing with the realization, but the professional musician in him rushed to fill the gap. A few minutes later, the program concluded to thunderous applause.

From his vantage point on the stage, Wendell could see the pastor walking up the steps. An image of Jesus rising up into the clouds flashed onto the screen.

Pastor John David Skipper stepped onto the stage and

shouted, "Alleluia! He has risen!" A chorus of amens erupted from the congregation. "Today we celebrate the most joyous of occasions," he said. "Ah, I see that confusion on your faces. You're wondering how this can be when our Lord was crucified?

"If you have your Bibles, turn with me to 1 John 4:9. 'In this was manifested the love of God toward us, because that God sent his only begotten Son into the world, that we might live through him.'

"Because of that love for His lambs, the Good Shepherd became the ultimate sacrifice. He suffered the vilest possible death out of love for us. He deemed us worthy of becoming joint heirs of His Father's Kingdom. Thank you, Jesus!" he cried out, again accompanied by the chorus of amens.

He turned and raised his hand toward the choir. "This group honored God and us today with this wonderful program. I know they worked many long and difficult hours to give Jesus their all. They didn't have to do it. They wanted to."

Wendell didn't understand why, but he'd never wanted to play a program of music as much as this one. The sacrifice of time in practice and rehearsal had been worth his effort. The pastor's next words took him by surprise.

"But their works won't get them into heaven," the pastor said. "Ephesians 2:8 says, "For by grace are ye saved through faith; and that not of yourselves: it is the gift of God.' Faith. Their belief that they serve a risen Lord who died for their sins, who washed them white as snow, will take them there."

FAITH in big bold print appeared on the screen. Where was his faith? Wendell wondered. Why had he rejected Jesus' gift? The image changed to two hands reaching out to each other.

"Have you made that choice?" Pastor Skipper asked. "If not, it's not too late. I'm going to ask the choir to lead us in 'Just as I Am.' Jesus wants you," he declared, pointing at the audience, "just as you are. He doesn't care what you've done in the past. He will forgive you if you just ask. It's a simple prayer that can lead you to a lifetime of joy. Repent and accept this enduring gift of love." With that, John David Skipper bowed his head.

Wendell didn't know the tune, so the choir sang a cappella. The congregation sat with their heads bowed, but he was aware of the people who approached the altar.

"*It's time, Wendell. Accept My love.*"

He couldn't be sure who spoke the words in his ear. He rose and took the first step, and soon he knelt at the altar. *Forgive me,* he pleaded silently. *Show me how to be the man You desire me to be. A man worthy of Your love.* The thoughts came faster and faster. He started slightly when a hand touched his shoulder. He looked at Jacob Truelove through tears of emotion and smiled.

"Do you understand the decision you're making?" Jacob asked.

Wendell shook his head. "No, sir. Not completely."

"Do you believe Jesus Christ died for your sins and was resurrected from the dead?" He paused. "Have you sinned against God and want to seek His forgiveness?" Another pause. "And do you plan to turn away from the past and invite Jesus to become Lord of your life?"

Wendell hesitated. The magnitude of the decision seemed overwhelming, and yet he knew he couldn't walk away. "I can only try to do my best."

"That's all He asks of us. Tell Him, Wendell, in your own words, what you plan to do."

He did, and freedom greater than he'd ever known filled him. Afterward Jacob patted his shoulder again and smiled widely.

"You've made a wise decision, son."

When Wendell looked up at Ophelia, she smiled and swiped away tears.

Every remaining doubt drifted away. He loved her. Whether he deserved her or not, she loved him.

After the service, people wanting to thank him for the music but more importantly, believers who wanted to extend the right hand of fellowship and welcome Wendell to the fold, delayed his departure. When her turn came, Ophelia threw her arms about his neck.

"I'm so happy for you."

He held her loosely, all the while wanting to pull her close and never let go. "Me, too. I'm not sure what happened, but I had to do this."

"The Holy Ghost guided you to make the right decision."

Wendell knew she spoke of the Trinity. "Looks like I'm going to be here for a while," he said, indicating the line that stretched down the aisle.

"Me, too," she said happily.

"I don't want to keep you from your lunch."

"You won't. This is more important than food."

He felt his jaw drop. He'd never thought he'd hear those words from her lips. "Ophelia Truelove considers standing next to me more important than food?"

She blushed. "Don't look at me like that. You're extremely important to me, Wendell."

He squeezed her hand, and she stepped aside so he could greet the next person. She remained by his side, thanking people for their compliments on her solo. "It wouldn't have happened without Wendell. Isn't he a wonderful pianist?"

People smiled and nodded, and her words lifted him higher than any self-pride.

❧

Their late lunch at the Trueloves' turned into a celebration of his decision.

"We had an honorary lunch for Russ when he made his decision," Val said, smiling at her fiancé.

"I'm glad to have my brother as my new brother in Christ," Russ agreed.

"It's all so new," Wendell commented. "I haven't even begun to understand this decision I've made."

"All in good time," Jacob said. "The most important thing is that you took that first step."

Later, Wendell went out to the barn with Jacob to check on Fancy. As her time approached, Wendell found himself growing more hopeful she would produce a winner. When she thrust her inquisitive head out of the stall, he ran his hand along the horse's neck. "Sir, I've wanted to ask how you can work in an industry and consider a major part of it a sin."

"It's not so cut-and-dried," Jacob said.

"When I step into this world, my thoughts turn to racing. How will I reconcile what I do with the choice I made this morning?" Wendell asked.

"God created these beautiful animals to run, and then He gave us this love of horses and put us right here in the midst of some of His most beautiful work."

Wendell couldn't dispute that.

"My problem with gambling relates to how it affected me personally," Jacob explained, tapping his chest as he emphasized the words. "I believe God put me here on this farm for a purpose. I pray and seek His guidance daily to understand what He'd have me do. Fear keeps me away from the tracks. I have my father's genes. Except for grace, I could be right where he is. Matthew 26:41 directs us to watch and pray that we don't enter into temptation.

"Just remember that you're a baby in Christ. You need to read your Bible, attend church, pray, and grow in Christ. As you grow, just as you did as a child, you learn to make judgment calls on what's right and wrong for you."

Wendell considered the choices of his childhood. They hadn't always been right choices. "What if I never make those calls?"

Jacob pulled an apple from his pocket and used his knife to cut it in half before feeding it to the mare. "God nudges you along. If He sees something standing in the way of you serving Him to your fullest, He prompts you to change. Back in November, He used a conversation between Val and Russ to show me I sinned against my father."

He didn't know Jacob that well, but he'd never seen anything that warranted the man calling himself a sinner. "Why would you think that?"

"I've been angry with him since I was a little boy. I didn't understand why he couldn't be like other dads. Then when he went to prison, I hated him for embarrassing us. He attached a stigma to our name that took years for us to overcome. We had to prove we weren't like him to regain people's respect. That's why my good name is important to me. I felt I earned it."

"Your anger was justified."

Jacob shook his head. "It's never justified, Wendell. My mother was the Sheridans' housekeeper. When she asked, Mr. Sheridan took me on. He taught me everything I know about horses and when he was satisfied I could do the job, he gave me the manager position. William Sheridan was a fine Christian man. I have him to thank for my salvation. He understood why I didn't want anything to do with the tracks and made it possible for me to stay away.

"I was determined my mother and siblings wouldn't suffer because of my father. I worked to help pay my brother's tuition. At times, the money was so tight I didn't know how I'd manage, but God made a way."

Jacob patted Fancy's head one last time and secured the door. They walked out to the golf cart. "That day Val told Russ he needed to seek your forgiveness," he said as they drove back toward the house, "he didn't think you'd listen, but she said he had to try. That got my attention. I'd decided my father didn't care and I shouldn't either. I appointed myself judge and jury. My father wasn't worthy of my love. Me," he declared, pointing to himself, "a simple man, for whom Christ hung on the cross and died, dared to consider he was better than his father.

"I won't say it's going to be easy. We went to visit him again and when I asked his forgiveness, he said he should be the one doing the asking. I felt so humbled."

Wendell understood the feeling. He hadn't given Russ much reason to love him, and yet his brother felt he'd wronged him. Even when he wanted nothing to do with religion, God had been at work. He'd salvaged another broken family and given them hope for the future.

They approached the house in silence, and Jacob parked

the cart. He hopped out and paused to look Wendell in the eye. "Trust God with your life, son. He'll help you make the right decisions."

As he listened to Jacob tell his family's story, Wendell understood what motivated this group. He believed Ophelia's desire to become a successful chef stemmed from this same need to help her family. No doubt she'd heard this story often, even achieved her goal with the intention of helping her younger siblings. He'd never experienced anything like this family's dedication. No doubt even now they grappled with how they could use the sudden influx of money to God's glory.

He came around the front of the cart and asked, "How would you feel about my asking Ophelia to marry me?"

Jacob stopped walking and turned to look at him. "You love her?"

With all his heart and soul. Wendell thought about that perfect-wife list. Had he given those items any thought since Ophelia came into his life? "Yes, sir, I do. I finally realized how much when I looked up at her today and knew my life would never be right without her."

Jacob clapped him on the back. "Son, you obviously made two life decisions today. And while I'm not against you asking for her hand, I advise you to pray before you act."

"I do have a lot to think about before I talk to her. I don't intend to push Ophelia," he allowed. "The decision will be hers. I'm concerned I'm too old for her."

"Opie could probably use someone to help settle her down. I love that girl, but she can be all over the place at times."

"I've never seen that side of Ophelia," Wendell defended. "In the time I've known her, she's done everything she set out to do. And that includes helping me find my way to God."

Jacob grinned. "I think you'll be good for my little girl, Wendell Hunter. Mighty good."

❧

Wendell and Opie walked out to the pavilion with the rest of the family trailing behind.

"Isn't it a glorious day?"

Opie twirled playfully, and Wendell found himself entranced by this side of her. He knew she didn't speak of the early spring weather with the newly budding trees and singing birds. Today's happiness was about successes and worthwhile decisions and just being together.

"Wonderful," he agreed, catching her hand and pulling her close.

"The kids," she murmured softly when he would have kissed her.

He groaned. He definitely had his work cut out for him in romancing this woman. He took her hand and said, "Let's go."

The day before, Rom and Heath hid candy-filled Easter eggs for the farm children's egg hunt that afternoon. Opie had extended the invitation to the Clarke children and any others from Hunter Farm who wanted to attend the event. She smiled as she looked upon the children sitting on the pavilion steps, waiting for the official announcement that they could find the eggs. They swung their Easter baskets restlessly, eager eyes looking around for the goodies.

"They're excited," she whispered.

"I can see."

"Did you ever have an egg hunt?"

"Daddy would hide the eggs. The real thing. We decorated boiled eggs with food coloring, wax pens, and decals. We had one specially marked lucky egg that generally got the finder a dollar."

"Wow, a whole dollar," he teased.

She tapped his arm. "There will be better prizes today," Opie said. "Heath and Rom hid eggs in all sorts of places. Some more obvious ones for the little kids and the not-so-obvious for the older ones."

Ronnie and Bonnie Clarke came running and grabbed her hands. "Ms. Truelove, we're going to hunt Easter eggs."

She smiled at their enthusiasm. "Yes, we are."

"Will you help us?"

Every adult present would be helping the children. "I will. Mr. Hunter will help, too. Won't you?" she asked, looking at Wendell.

"Definitely," he agreed with a twinkle in his eye as he declared, "My team is going to find the most eggs today."

Ronnie broke away from her and went over to take Wendell's hand. "Can I be on your team?"

"What's your name, son?" he asked.

"Ronnie."

"Well, Ronnie, I think we should get over there, so we can be the first ones to start looking." He winked at her before they took off running across the pavilion yard.

"Come on, Bonnie," Opie said with a laugh. "We can't let them beat us."

Minutes later, all the children carried baskets piled high with their bounty.

"Look, Daddy," Ronnie said to the young man who came to retrieve his children. "Mr. Hunter helped me find all these."

Ronald Clarke's skin turned ruddy with embarrassment as his gaze shifted to his employer. "Thank you, Mr. Hunter. And thanks for helping me out of my predicament."

Wendell reached out to shake Ronald's hand. "It was my pleasure. You have two fine children. Take care of them."

"Yes, sir, I will."

"Ronald," he called when father and son started to walk away. The man looked back. "Next time you need investment advice, come see me. I know a thing or two about making money."

Opie slipped her arm about Wendell's, smiling up at him as she whispered, "Thank you."

sixteen

Before he left that night, Wendell invited Ophelia to join him for lunch the following day. She agreed. He'd given his staff the day off for the holiday and decided to pick up items for a picnic and take her out to the farm. When he arrived to pick her up, she wore pink capri pants with a white sleeveless blouse. "You might want to take a jacket." The spring days could get a little chilly at times.

"Got it," she said, taking a knit coat from the coatrack in the entry hall. "Where are we going?"

Wendell didn't plan to use the word surprise. "I thought we'd have a picnic at my favorite place on the farm. Sound good?"

"Perfect."

He walked her out to a Jeep and waited as she climbed inside. "I thought about riding out there, but the Jeep is just as good."

A few minutes later, he parked at the perfect vantage point to look out over Hunter Farm. Rolling hills of blue-grass spread before them, mature trees providing shade. Trails of black fences surrounded the area, some containing horses. They could see the house in the distance. Wendell took a blanket from the backseat. Ophelia indicated an area, and he shook out the blanket and let it settle on the ground. She helped pull out the corners.

"I have no idea what's in here," he said as he set the basket in the corner.

"You should have asked me to put something together."

"You deserved a holiday, too." He stood and held out his hand, "Let's take a walk."

Ophelia took his hand, and he boosted her to her feet. He pulled her closer.

"Still reeling from yesterday?" she asked as they strolled along.

"Some. I'm handling it with prayer. Your dad calls them life-changing decisions. I'm sure it will take time to sort out the particulars. But I plan to attend your church, and the pastor mentioned a new Christians' class."

"Call me if you feel the need to talk," she told him.

"That's why I asked you over today."

Her brows lifted. "What did you have on your mind?"

Wendell noticed her struggle to be as casual as possible with the question. "You."

She stopped and looked up at him. "Me? What do you mean?"

"There were tears in your eyes yesterday. Was that because you were joyous over my decision to follow Christ, or do you feel something more for me?"

"You know I care about you, Wendell. I've never made any secret of that. And yes, I am happy for you."

"Friend happy?"

A suggestion of annoyance touched her face. "What are you asking, Wendell?"

"Do you love me?"

"Yes, I do. Despite your insistence that you're not right for me," she said with a defiant smile. "I care for you a great deal."

"I came to the same realization yesterday. I love you and hoped you felt the same for me."

Her eyes brightened with pleasure. "So what are we going to do about it?"

"Get to know each other. I think I already know a few things about you. Like how you love your family and your career. About your work. . ."

"Okay, Wendell," she interrupted. "I wasn't about to tell you this when you said there could be no us, but I decided awhile back that you were more important than my work," she admitted in a rush of words. "That doesn't mean I'll ever stop cooking. I will prepare meals for my family, but I'd give up my career for you."

Her admission knocked the breath out of him. "Why?"

"I think you need to be your wife's focus. Being a middle child wasn't easy. I always felt like I needed to compete with my siblings for my parents' love. I know that wasn't the case, but I wouldn't want you to feel anything is more important to me than you, and I'm afraid you might feel that way about my career."

He doubted he could love her more than he did in that moment. "I might have felt that way before I understood your work is a part of you. You like the compliments and you deserve them. I think you do what you do because a completed job shows you can take a project to completion. I won't ask you to give that up."

"What are you saying?"

"We support each other in the things that make us happy. We make time in our busy schedules for each other. And when things go as I hope they will, you'll be at my side forever."

She threw her arms about his waist and hugged him. Wendell looped his arms about her back. He leaned to kiss her, savoring the sweetness that was Ophelia Truelove. "Will it be uncomfortable for you to socialize with the people you've cooked for?"

"I feel your friends respect me for who I am, and I doubt any of them would ever say no to a meal at our house," she said, flashing him a cheeky grin.

He laughed. "Now that I understand about the races, I won't ask you to do anything that might make you uncomfortable."

"I enjoyed the races, Wendell. It's exciting to witness those horses doing what they were born to do." She giggled and said, "When I was admiring Dell Air before the race, I felt he was thinking 'Yeah, I know I look good.'"

"It's the stallion in him."

"I felt I let Daddy down by doing something he asked us not to do."

"I'm surprised he didn't say something to me about taking you."

"Daddy understands you, Wendell."

Wendell hoped so. He wanted the respect of the man he

admired so much. "Jacob says I'm a babe in Christ. He says that as I grow in my faith, I'll learn what God wants me to do."

"You will. Let's go check out that basket. All this fresh air and sunshine has given me an appetite."

❧

Wendell embraced the idea of courtship, and the more time he spent with Ophelia, the more he realized a woman with the qualities he'd thought he wanted would have bored him to death in no time. He recalled her insistence that God was at work in their lives and accepted it was true.

He took her to his social engagements, and Ophelia provided him with the family he'd always wanted. He spent nearly as many evenings in the Truelove home as he did in his own. They explored the things they had in common and enjoyed being together. They even went horseback riding frequently.

Three weeks later, Wendell invited Val and Russ over for dinner and they accepted. Ophelia worked that night and he'd thought about waiting until she could attend, but he wanted their opinion on his plan.

"I have some things I thought you might like for your place," Wendell told Russ after dinner.

He indicated the portrait of Russ's mother and another of their father and Russ's mother. A similar portrait hung in the hallway. There were boxes of photos. "I copied the ones that meant something to me, but they're part of your childhood and I think you should have them."

Russ looked somewhat overwhelmed. "Please don't think it's my intention to remove you from Hunter Farm," Wendell said. "I hope you'll always think of it as your home."

"I will. I have fond memories of my childhood home, but it's only right that it belong to you and your children. Besides, I've come to think of home in a different way lately."

"Certain things do lose their significance in the greater scheme of things," Wendell agreed. As he spent time reading his Bible, Wendell accepted that worldly possessions weren't as important as he'd once believed. "I hope our kids will play here together in a way we never did."

Val smiled at him and asked, "The thought pleases you, doesn't it?"

"A great deal. I haven't been much of a brother, but I intend to change."

They moved into the drawing room. "Val, I plan to propose to your sister, and I'd like to surprise her. Will you help?"

"What did you have in mind?"

"I thought we'd have a dinner party for your family, and I'd ask Ophelia to prepare the meal. Give her free rein to try some of the things your mother won't let her cook at home."

"You plan to make us guinea pigs?" Val teased.

"Ophelia knows how far she can go. I'm asking her to be my hostess."

"I'm sure she'll love playing lady of the manor, but she'll probably think it's a weird request."

He chuckled. "It's a twofold plan. She gets to do what she loves and then after dinner, I perform a piece I wrote for her. The first music I've written since Dad died. It's entitled 'Ophelia's Song.'"

"Oh wow," Val said. "She'll love that."

"After the music, I'll ask her to marry me."

"Have you talked to Daddy?"

Wendell nodded. "We discussed the age difference, and he feels it's not an issue."

"Is the age thing the only problem you have?" Russ asked.

"You know my background, Russ. I feel life with Ophelia will make a difference. I appreciate the way she's always so happy and desires to see others happy as well. She makes me laugh and deals well with my sarcasm. We both like to do things spur of the moment. That's why I think she'll like my proposal."

"Sounds almost as romantic as mine," Val said. "The pavilion is available, and the weather is really beautiful if you'd like to do this outside."

"No," Wendell said with a shake of his head. "That was

your fantasy. It's better if we come here. I need my piano, and Ophelia needs my kitchen."

"I think she knew from the moment she laid eyes on you in that magazine that you would play a major role in her life. There were times I regretted taking her to that bachelor auction."

"She let me know how she felt, but I fought her," Wendell admitted.

"Believe me, I know. She was miserable. When she suggested we ask you to play for the cantata, I thought she'd lost her mind. I thought it might be her way of staying in your life. She didn't deny it."

"I was hooked from the time I listened to the CD. I had no idea how I'd find the time, but that music filled me heart and soul. I'm thankful she asked."

"She thought she could change you with God's help."

"She did."

"You challenge her. She wouldn't give up even though she had no idea how to reach you."

Wendell smiled. "I couldn't fight her. She may be tiny, but she's huge when it comes to love. If you have time, I'd like to show you what I'm planning for her engagement gift. We'll need to ride into Paris."

Val looked at Russ and he shrugged. "Sure."

❧

Wendell parked in front of one of the old storefronts and pulled a key from his pocket. He opened the door, turned on the lights, and gestured for Val to go first.

"She's going to love this," she exclaimed after they examined the building.

"I know she's wanted her own kitchen for a long time." Opie had told him she wanted to teach women to prepare tasty nutritious meals for their families. "I think she can renovate this building to serve her purpose."

"She has the pavilion kitchen now," Russ offered.

"But she'll need to be in Paris for the cooking school."

"What happens if she refuses?"

"If she does, I'll rent her this place at a ridiculously low price. I want to see her achieve her dreams, too. You won't tell her, will you?"

"I don't think so," Val said with a little laugh. "She sent me out into the freezing cold to turn out the lights knowing Russ planned to propose. I'm going to enjoy seeing her surprise when it happens to her."

Wendell shook his head. "You two and your pranks."

"All in good fun. You and Russ might do the same one day."

Wendell grinned. "I hope so."

"I'll keep that in mind," Russ said.

After they locked up and returned to the vehicle, Val asked, "Do you think you'd have met if I hadn't talked her into the bachelor auction?"

"As Opie tells me all the time, God is in control."

Val smiled at Russ. "God does work in wonderful ways. I never dreamed He'd answer my prayer and then send Russ to help me achieve my goal."

Russ pointed at her and said, "He sent you to help me find Him."

"And He used Ophelia to bring me home," Wendell said.

❧

The next day Wendell drove over to the pavilion where he knew Ophelia was preparing for a party that night. She whipped off the net that covered her hair when he walked in and brushed her hands over her apron. "Wendell, hi."

"Do you have a minute?"

"If you don't mind talking while I work."

"I want you to help me host a party for your family at my house. I've enjoyed their hospitality many times, and I'd like to return the favor. I want you to prepare the meal, too. I'll give Jean-Pierre the night off."

She looked puzzled by his request. "Let me get this straight. You want me to come to your house and prepare a meal my family might or might not like and then cohost the dinner?"

Wendell nodded. "That's what I'm suggesting. The two of

us entertaining your family at a dinner party." He noted a spark of interest in the green gaze.

"And I get to serve whatever I want?"

"Whatever you want," Wendell agreed.

"When do you want to do this?"

"What about Friday night two weeks?"

"Sounds wacky but I'm on board."

"It wouldn't be any different if Jean-Pierre prepared the meal. The food could still be outside their comfort zone."

She grinned. "I'll make sure it's food they'll eat, but I'm going to put a new spin on the menu just because I can."

≥●

On the night before the dinner party, Wendell pushed back the overwhelming emotion as he practiced the piece he'd written. He thanked God for bringing Ophelia into his life and making it possible for them to be together.

She arrived with her supplies early the next morning. He stopped in to find her consumed with her lists, systematically working her way through the menu, while her assistants worked on the lists she'd given them. Just before their guests arrived, he went into the kitchen again. "Everything okay in here?"

"Time isn't a luxury in the kitchen, Wendell. If service is in minutes, the food must be ready. It's not like I can ask everyone to wait."

"In other words, you're telling me to get lost?"

"Only with the greatest of love," she agreed with a sweet smile.

Val and Russ were the first to arrive. "Ready for tonight?" she asked softly.

Wendell nodded. "I'm not as sure about Ophelia. I'm afraid she'll be too tired to enjoy herself."

"Cooking energizes Opie."

"Why don't you see if she has time to change before dinner?" Wendell suggested.

"She'd rather wear her chef's jacket than anything else."

"For her proposal?"

Val shrugged. "With Opie, you never know. A photo of you proposing to her in chef whites and a toque would probably make it into the paper as your engagement photo."

"You think she'll choose those for our wedding?"

"Oh, no way. I've seen her favorite bridal gown and it's fantastic."

"That's good to know," Wendell said with a pleased smile. He looked forward to seeing Ophelia in her wedding dress. Of course, he needed to propose first.

She did change and dinner was extraordinary.

"What have you done?" Wendell asked when they served the appetizer of fried Louisiana shrimp balls.

She only winked and shrugged.

The dinner menu consisted of game hens with cornbread stuffing, green beans, and hot yeast rolls and butter. Chocolate mousse with raspberry sauce finished it off to perfection.

"What do you call these?" Cy asked as he held up a green bean with his fork.

"Beans?" Opie said, her tongue-in-cheek response gaining his childish reaction.

"They're not. You call them 'hairy covers.'"

Opie grinned and pronounced the term properly. "*Haricots vert.*"

"Man, you chefs take something easy and make it hard."

"Actually we take something simple and make it delectable," she corrected.

"My little girl knows how to cook," Jacob said. "I'm proud of you, Opie."

"To Ophelia," Wendell said, raising his glass in a toast.

After dinner, they moved into the drawing room.

"You really did a wonderful job with the Easter program," Cindy said, running a hand over the piano as she passed. "You're incredibly talented."

"Thank you," Wendell said. "I thought I might play a little something I wrote. I dabbled at writing music but lost the desire after my dad died. Recently I've been inspired by a young woman who turned my life upside down."

Ophelia was intrigued. He could see it in her eyes. "This woman challenged me in ways I couldn't imagine. She told me life could be better. Then she helped me find my way to that new life."

He stood and held out his hand to Ophelia. She took it, and Wendell led her over to the armchair by the piano. He seated himself at the bench. "I call this 'Ophelia's Song.'"

His gaze never left hers as he played the song from his heart. Tears streamed down her cheeks. When he finished, Wendell pulled a box from his pocket and went down on bended knee before her. "I love you, Ophelia. More than I can say. This may not be the most spectacular way of sharing that. . ."

"You wrote a song for me," she interrupted.

He grinned at her exuberance.

"I wanted you to know how I felt." He popped open the box to show her the ring. His mother's ring. He'd found it among her jewelry in the attic and thought that one day his bride might want to wear the three-carat pear-shaped diamond. "Ophelia, will you marry me?"

"Only if you stop calling me Ophelia."

Startled by her response, Wendell broke into laughter. Soon the others joined in.

"We've got a dilemma, my love. I don't see an Opie when I look at you."

"I suppose I could get used to my love," she said. "Yes, Wendell, I'll marry you." She held his face in her hands and declared, "I love you, and there's nothing I want more than to be your wife."

He kissed her, not caring that their family looked on as they sealed their commitment to a future together.

seventeen

"Ready?" Jacob Truelove asked.

Opie could only nod. Last night when Wendell kissed her good night, he'd requested that she remember how much he loved her when he played "Ophelia's Song" today just for her. As if she could ever forget. He'd even gone to the extreme of giving her a storefront for her business. She'd willingly give up her career for him, but his action spoke of his faith that she would be everything he needed in a wife.

"Three of you married in one day," Jacob said. "It's almost more than a man can take in."

Opie shared her father's amazement. "I told you we had plans for you and that tux."

"Yeah, you did. I suppose Rom and Stephanie will make me wear it to their wedding."

Stephanie had flown in over the weekend and though he hadn't wanted to take away from their happiness, Rom announced at lunch that she agreed to become his wife. They reveled in his joy and teased him about being too late to join them.

"Admit it, Daddy, you'll be glad to have us out of your hair."

"Sweet, sweet Opie, when you have babies of your own you'll realize that's impossible."

Babies. Hard to imagine, but she looked forward to having a family with Wendell. She'd realized that a career and following your dreams meant nothing compared to love.

"You're grown and very shortly you'll be married, but I'd never be glad to be without any of you. I praised God the day your mother told me you were on the way, and I praise Him today for your happiness and well-being. But I am not losing three children," Jacob said. "I'm gaining three. With your vows, Jane, Russ, and Wendell become my daughter and sons as well.

They're as much a part of our family as my own blood."

"Wendell said he loves my family almost as much as he loves me," Opie said.

"Don't feel threatened by that, sweetheart. No one knows more than you do how tough his life has been. He needs a family to love and care for him. We'll be there to back you up."

"Thanks, Daddy. I wouldn't have it any other way."

❧

When Wendell proposed, Cy said they might as well get married on the same day and have the Truelove Triple Crown of weddings. Val had asked Heath and Jane to share her day and immediately said she'd love it if Opie and Wendell did the same. Wendell joked that planning a parachute jump in a windstorm would be easier than one event for three couples but admitted the Trueloves did weddings in style.

The weddings would follow the order of their engagements. Each bride would have one attendant to help with her dress and flowers. Each groom would have a best man. Their minister would marry each couple and then they would remain on their pedestal, which would slide to the side and rotate the next couple to the altar. He didn't want to guess what Val paid for that piece of equipment. Val, Jane, and Ophelia pleaded with him to play for the weddings. After he played "Ophelia's Song," he would turn the piano over to someone else for Ophelia's wedding march.

Last night, after the rehearsal and dinner, they left the group to stroll along the lighted pathway about the pavilion.

"Fancy's baby came last night," she told him. "It was a girl. I'm sorry."

Wendell lifted her hand to his lips. "I'm not. Your dad got his girl. I got mine." Ophelia smiled at him. "And I'm sure ours won't be the only Hunter/Truelove union. Your dad and I have plans to make our own place in Thoroughbred horse history."

"With God's help, I know we'll accomplish wonderful things."

Later after he'd said his good nights and gone home, Ophelia's promise stayed with him. The very idea that she would make him the happiest man alive in a few hours kept him awake. Wendell went into the kitchen and found a small basket on the island. He smiled at the coffee-hot cocoa mix in the heart mug and a sleeve of her delicious cookies. As he waited for the milk to heat, Wendell looked at the tag on the package, finding that she'd written him a love note. He grinned, sending up a special prayer of thanks for Ophelia.

As Wendell enjoyed the comfort of the hot drink and cookies, he went over the schedule for the next day. He'd invited the grooms, their best men, Jacob, and the younger Truelove boys to join him for breakfast the next morning. After that, they'd dress and head over to the pavilion.

The morning passed in a flash. The three men prayed together before they took their places.

Not a tremble, Wendell thought as his hands moved over the keyboard. But then he played "Ophelia's Song" and a fine nervousness touched him. "Please, God," he whispered, "make me the man she deserves."

Wendell left the piano and grinned when Russ gave him the thumbs-up. He felt honored to share this wonderful family with his brother. He took his place with his friend Leo at his side. When Ophelia stepped into view, every thought in his head went away.

"Breathe, man."

Following Leo's instruction, he sucked in a deep breath and managed a smile. All those years he'd mistakenly thought that winning a Triple Crown would be the ultimate. It couldn't compare to this. To say she looked stunning would be an understatement. Though it was his first time seeing the dress, Ophelia teased him with words like beaded lace and mermaid. All he could think was that she'd packaged the beauty of her love and was about to present him with the gift. Wendell hugged Jacob and took Ophelia's hand in his. They stepped up onto the pedestal, and her cousin Jennifer adjusted her dress. As Ophelia held on to his arm, the feeling of rightness overwhelmed him. Ophelia told him she'd planned for her future and career, but not for love. She'd said she now understood how senseless her life would have been without him. Wendell understood precisely what she meant.

She admitted the true challenge she'd confronted hadn't been changing him. It had been changing herself, understanding that she couldn't do anything because the only plans that triumphed were those of God. She'd learned that the hard way when she'd become convinced she could change Wendell with God's help. As it turned out, God used her to accomplish His plan.

Wendell had never imagined he would overcome the anger and hurt that had filled him for so long. Now as he stood beside her, he experienced a second great joy—that of becoming one with the woman he loved.

"Do you, Wendell, take Ophelia to be your lawfully wedded wife?" Pastor Skipper asked.

Ophelia grinned and whispered, "Are you up to the challenge?"

"God is," Wendell said softly before adding his own loud, emphatic, "I do."

epilogue

A little more than two weeks later, the entire family gathered to watch a news feature that ran while the three couples were on their honeymoons. The well-known face of the reporter who interviewed Val all those months before flashed on the screen. She stood just outside the pavilion.

"Today this reporter had the privilege of attending an event such as I've never before witnessed. The wedding venue site resonated with love as three couples shared their joy with family and friends. When asked, Valentine Truelove Hunter said that she'd never imagined how wonderful it would be to marry the man of her dreams in the beauty of the Kentucky countryside.

"Darcy, the youngest Truelove child, referred to the event as the Triple Crown of weddings and this reporter would agree. I found it to be among the unique experiences of my life. A beautiful venue, three beautiful brides, three handsome grooms, a bevy of equally gorgeous attendants along with the sweetest flower girl I've ever seen, delicious food, and count 'em, three beautiful wedding cakes." The camera went to the three individually designed cakes. "Every bride's dream.

"The remaining single twin, Romeo, which rumor has it is newly engaged this week, summed it up best in his toast." The scene flipped to a shot of Rom standing atop the pavilion stage.

"Today I have the honor of toasting three very precious people in my life—my sisters, Val and Opie, and my twin Heath. Each of you have found your soul mate and committed to love and honor each other. May you always have joy in your lives and may you always dream Bluegrass Dreams."

A chorus of "hear, hear!" rose up in the Paris countryside.

The camera went back to the reporter. "Your Wedding Place has quite a future here in our community, and after this experience I expect we'll see many more perfect weddings at this spectacular venue."

A Letter To Our Readers

Dear Reader:

In order that we might better contribute to your reading enjoyment, we would appreciate your taking a few minutes to respond to the following questions. We welcome your comments and read each form and letter we receive. When completed, please return to the following:

Fiction Editor
Heartsong Presents
PO Box 719
Uhrichsville, Ohio 44683

1. Did you enjoy reading *Opie's Challenge* by Terry Fowler?
   ❏ Very much! I would like to see more books by this author!
   ❏ Moderately. I would have enjoyed it more if

   _____
   _____
   _____

2. Are you a member of **Heartsong Presents**? ❏ Yes ❏ No
   If no, where did you purchase this book? _____
   _____

3. How would you rate, on a scale from 1 (poor) to 5 (superior), the cover design? _____

4. On a scale from 1 (poor) to 10 (superior), please rate the following elements.

   ____ Heroine   ____ Plot
   ____ Hero   ____ Inspirational theme
   ____ Setting   ____ Secondary characters

5. These characters were special because? _____

_____

_____

6. How has this book inspired your life? _____

_____

_____

7. What settings would you like to see covered in future
   Heartsong Presents books? _____

_____

_____

8. What are some inspirational themes you would like to see
   treated in future books? _____

_____

_____

9. Would you be interested in reading other **Heartsong
   Presents** titles? ❏ Yes ❏ No

10. Please check your age range:

    ❏ Under 18   ❏ 18–24

    ❏ 25–34   ❏ 35–45

    ❏ 46–55   ❏ Over 55

Name _____

Occupation _____

Address _____

City, State, Zip _____

E-mail _____

Heartsong

HEARTSONG PRESENTS TITLES AVAILABLE NOW:

Presents